He made her laugh.

Earlier she'd tried to cover her amusement with sarcasm, but lately Will had a cute way of getting back at her. She felt like a kid again, rather than the dignified woman she'd considered herself to be.

"You're on," she said. "If I love it here, I owe you something big. A seven-course dinner or…" She faltered, realizing she was having a good time.

"I'll make that decision when I collect," he said with a wink over his shoulder.

Above the roar of the engine, he hollered back his usual witty comments, his youthful spirit so evident as they soared across the snow. Youthful, yet he had depth, too, Christine had noticed. She watched the tenderness he had for her grandmother, and Christine couldn't help but noti̶̶̶̶ ̶̶̶̶w he studied her. She didn't th̶̶̶̶̶̶̶̶̶̶̶̶̶̶̶̶red her out yet, but h̶

Books by Gail Gaymer Martin

Love Inspired

Upon a Midnight Clear #117
Secrets of the Heart #147
A Love for Safekeeping #161
Loving Treasures #177
Loving Hearts #199
Easter Blessings #202
   "The Butterfly Garden"
The Harvest #223
   "All Good Gifts"

Loving Ways #231
Loving Care #239
Adam's Promise #259
Loving Promises #291
Loving Feelings #303
Loving Tenderness #323
†*In His Eyes* #361
†*With Christmas in His Heart* #373

*Loving

Steeple Hill Books

The Christmas Kite
That Christmas Feeling
   "Christmas Moon"
Finding Christmas

GAIL GAYMER MARTIN

lives in Michigan with her husband, Bob, her dearest friend and greatest supporter. She feels blessed to be writing stories that touch people's hearts and share God's mercy and forgiveness. Friends often tease her that they're afraid to share life experiences with her. They have asked, "Will this be in your next novel?" Sometimes it is.

Gail is multipublished in nonfiction and over thirty works of fiction. Her novels have received numerous awards: a Booksellers Best in 2005, a Holt Medallion in 2001 and 2003, the Texas Winter Rose 2003, the American Christian Romance Writers 2002 Book of the Year Award and the *Romantic Times BOOKclub* Reviewers Choice as best Love Inspired novel of 2002. At present, over one million copies of her books are in print.

When not behind her computer, Gail enjoys a busy life—traveling, presenting writers' workshops, speaking at churches, business groups, libraries and civic centers. She is a soloist and member of her church's choir, as well as a ringer in their handbell and hand-chime choirs. She also sings with the Detroit Lutheran Singers.

She enjoys hearing from her readers. Write to her at P.O. Box 7600063, Lathrup Village, MI 48076 or at gail@gailmartin.com. Visit her Web site at www.gailmartin.com.

GAIL GAYMER MARTIN

WITH *Christmas* IN HIS *Heart*

Steeple
Hill®

Published by Steeple Hill Books™

STEEPLE HILL BOOKS

Steeple
Hill®

ISBN-13: 978-0-373-87405-7
ISBN-10:   0-373-87405-7

WITH CHRISTMAS IN HIS HEART

www.SteepleHill.com

Printed in U.S.A.

In his heart a man plans his course,
but the Lord determines his steps.
—*Proverbs* 16:9

Acknowledgments

A huge thank-you to Kay Hoppenrath, a year-round resident of Mackinac Island, who kindly provided me with so much wonderful information about the island life, especially in winter, so that my story could be real. Though I tried to be accurate, I occasionally took a novelist's prerogative. Mackinac Island has given me and all visitors wonderful memories. It is a special place that takes me back in time to a world we don't know anymore. What a blessing. Also, thanks to bookseller Tamara Tomac, who found Kay as a willing ear for my questions.

To Shelly Gaponik, my niece, who helped me with my snowmobile lingo. Hopefully I got it right.

Thanks to physician Mel Hodde and writer friends Marta Perry and Carol Steward, who provided me with accurate stroke information.

As always to my husband, Bob, who is my right arm and my dearest friend and who provided me with stained-glass information.

Chapter One

Christine Powers clung to the railing of the ferry, chilled to the bone yet hot under the collar, a cliché her father often used.

Her father. Her parents. How could she begrudge them an anniversary cruise? Yet while they swayed in the tropic breezes, she had been trapped into this freezing trip to Mackinac Island to care for her grandmother.

Important projects were piled on her desk back in Southfield. Her clients' deadlines had been pushed back as much as they could be so she could make the trip that had rankled her from the moment her father had asked.

She loved her grandmother. She loved her parents. But she also loved her career, and putting it in jeopardy hadn't sat well with her.

The ferry bumped against the pier, giving her a jolt, and Christine watched a crew member toss a line to a dockhand. Her gaze moved up the long wooden pier to the island town. Through the swirling snowflakes she could see Fort Mackinac sitting proudly on a hill, its white concrete walls providing a barricade when, hundreds of years earlier, many nations entered the Michigan waters to take over the island.

In the summer, Christine loved Mackinac Island. She loved its history and landscape and the uniqueness that captured tourists from all over. But she didn't love it now—not when she felt mired in the midst of too many projects that needed completion. She had advertising copy to edit, two ad campaigns to finalize and a new client to impress. The Dorset account would make her shine in the eyes of her firm.

A ragged sigh escaped, leaving a billow of white breath hanging on the air. She lifted her shoulders and grasped her carry-on bag, determined to get through the next few days.

When she heard the clang of the gangway, she maneuvered through the expansive benches toward the front of the boat to disembark. As she neared, she surveyed the prow, where she hoped to see her other bag, but the area stood bare.

A crewman flagged her forward, and she stepped onto the slippery ramp, clutching the railing until her feet hit the pier.

"Careful," a crewman called.

She muttered a thank-you and had taken two steps forward when her foot slipped on the icy planking.

She skidded, her arms flailing while her carry-on bag landed on the pier. A hand grasped her arm to steady her, and the crew member who'd warned her gave her a knowing grin.

She managed a smile—better than screaming—and retrieved her bag. She took guarded steps toward the ferry exit, where she eyed a workman unloading the luggage. She looked through the feathery flakes, praying hers was there and not left back in Mackinaw City.

If she weren't so stressed, the snowfall would be appealing. The soft flakes drifted past her, twirling on the frigid breeze that streamed off the straits. Why would anyone want to live on an island so isolated in the winter? By the beginning of January their only escape would be by air until the ice bridge was ready.

A shiver ran through her as she stepped beneath the enclosure and reached the ferry's cargo. Her worry eased when she spotted her suitcase. She set down her small bag and tugged at her luggage beneath the other baggage.

"Let me help."

Her focus shifted to the stranger who'd stepped beside her. She jumped at his closeness, then was thrown off guard by his wide grin.

"Thanks. I have it." She gave another determined tug and settled the suitcase beside her, pulled up the handle and tried to connect the carry-on bag to the larger piece.

The man didn't move from the spot. He shook his head as he watched, then gave a chuckle when her carry-on slipped to the ground.

If she hadn't been so irked, she would have enjoyed his smile, but his laughter rubbed her the wrong way. "That wasn't funny. My laptop's in there."

"Sorry," he said, looking less than sorry with his boyish grin and snapping dark eyes. "I assume you're Christine Powers. I've been waiting for you."

She stopped short. "I'm Christine, but who are you, if I might ask?"

He drew back and looked surprised. "I thought you knew I was coming for you. I'm Will. Will Lambert. I board with your grandmother."

"You board with my grandmother? Since when?"

"For the past year."

She controlled her jaw from sagging a foot. "No one told me."

He shrugged. "I guess you'll have to trust me. I'm trusting you're actually Christine Powers."

That made her laugh despite the cold penetrating her leather gloves. "I wasn't expecting anyone to meet me," she said, anxious to get away from the bitter wind. "I'd planned to take a taxi."

"Then you have your dream come true."

She squinted at him, wondering if he were loony or being humorous. He gestured toward the street. "The taxi's waiting. I offered to meet you because your grandmother thought you'd have a ton of luggage."

He grasped the handle of her large case and reached for the smaller one, but she clutched it as if it held her life's treasures. "I'll carry this myself."

"Okay," he said, shrugging. "The carriage is this way." He took a step forward and looked back to make sure she was following.

Carriage? The question was fleeting. What else? The unique island had no motorized conveyances except for a couple of emergency vehicles and snowmobiles when there was enough snowfall. Horse and carriage was a common mode of transportation.

Her limbs tensed as she checked the ground for icy patches. Christine eyed the man ahead of her. He had broad shoulders and an easy gait, as if he knew who he was and liked himself. She would enjoy having that feeling, but at times, she wasn't sure she knew who she was. The boarder had a casual manner, sort of a rough gallantry like a young John Wayne. She could almost picture him in a tilted Stetson.

When Will stepped from under the covering onto the sidewalk, Christine stopped beneath the enclosure and looked at snow that quickly dissipated to slush beneath the feet of the horses.

Will turned toward her as if wondering why she'd been dawdling, but she didn't hurry. Let him wait. She studied him, watching his breath puff in a white mist. He wore a dark leather jacket and a dark blue scarf around his neck. He had a youthful look yet a face that appeared seasoned by life.

Christine had learned to study people first and

form an opinion before she let down her guard. She'd learned to analyze her clients at the firm. Sadly, she hadn't always been as astute at judging people as she was today.

Stepping from beneath the shelter, she turned her attention to Main Street, where buggies lined the road—hotel shuttles, private conveyances and taxis, like the one that would take her to her grandmother's. The town had already captured the feeling of Christmas. Large wreaths with bright red ribbons hung from the old-fashioned streetlights, and the dusting of snow created a Christmas-card setting.

The scent of winter sharpened the air and softened the scent of horse muck that steamed from the cold ground. She recoiled again, amazed she'd agreed to do this "little favor" for her parents.

As the driver loaded her case behind the seat, the horse's flank quivered, and it stomped its foot as if ready to be on its way. Will reached for her smaller case, and this time she relinquished it. He handed it to the driver, who put it behind the seat with her other bag. He told the driver where they were headed, then offered to assist her.

She placed her hand in his, feeling his warm palm and long fingers clasping hers to give her a lift into the buggy.

The cab tipped as Will joined her and pulled a lap robe over her legs. "This will keep you warmer."

The driver looked over his shoulder through the front window. "Ready?" he asked.

"We're all set," Will called. When he settled against the seat, his eyes sought hers, and she must have grimaced, because his look softened. "You'll get used to this. It takes a while. Modern conveniences are a habit, not a necessity."

He said it with a self-assured tone that seemed patronizing. Christine liked conveniences. In fact, she liked luxuries, and she wasn't planning to apologize for her taste.

The horse jerked forward and moved down Huron Street, its clip-clop rhythm rocking the floorboards. Her shoulder hit Will's, and he shifted. A cool spot filled the space, and she almost wished he would have stayed closer.

The driver snapped the reins again and the horse picked up its pace. She studied the scene, noting many shops appeared closed as they trotted past, their interiors dark and the displays gone from the windows. A wreath on the door gave sign that the restaurant was open, and more Christmas decor brightened the pharmacy and grocery store.

Will was quiet, and she wondered what he had on his mind.

He glanced at her, as if realizing she'd been looking at him. "Life here is different from the big city. Can you imagine not having to lock your doors?"

"Not really," she said, turning toward the scenery.

But her quiet didn't stop him. He talked about the community while she viewed the passing landscape.

She didn't want to get caught up in his lighthearted prattle. She'd been miserable about coming here, and she planned to stay that way. Her attitude jolted her. She was being childish, but right now she didn't care.

Ahead, Huron Street veered right past the visitor's center. Christine viewed the wide lawn of the fort now hidden beneath a fine blanket of snow. The jingle of the horse's bells set her in a holiday mood, despite her opposition to being here.

The driver pulled the reins, and they turned up Fort Road. As they climbed Fort Hill, the wind nipped at their backs and sent a chill down Christine's spine.

"Cold?" Will asked, tucking the blanket more securely around her legs. "If you move closer to me, I'll block the wind."

She noted his masculine frame and, though feeling odd nestled beside a perfect stranger, she shifted toward him, grateful for the offer. When she moved, he slid his arm around her shoulders.

For a fleeting moment she drew away, but the wind lunged across her again. Reconsidering, she settled beside him. Pride and independence held no value if she froze to death.

Steam billowed from the horse's nostrils as it trotted along, its hooves clopping on the asphalt road and breaking the deep silence.

"How long will you be here?"

"Only a week or so." Her breath ballooned like a white cloud.

"That's right. Your parents went on a cruise."

She eyed him, wondering what else he knew about her family. "A Caribbean cruise."

"Warm weather in the Caribbean. Sounds nice, although I like winter," he said. As a second thought, he added, "Nice you're filling in for them."

Nice probably wasn't the word. She'd resented it, but she'd come. "They're celebrating their fortieth wedding anniversary."

Will drew her tighter against his shoulder. "Forty. That's great. Your parents are nice Christian people."

"They are," she said, feeling on edge again. Her Christian upbringing had taught her to honor her parents and show compassion, but while her parents followed those rules, she wasn't always very good at it.

The road veered to the right, past the governor's summer residence, then at the fork, the driver turned onto Cupid's Pathway. When she saw the house ahead of her, she pulled away from Will's protection, hoping to regain her composure.

"Here we are," he said, as the driver reined in the horse beside the lovely Victorian home. The house tugged at her memories—summer memories, she reminded herself.

Will jumped off the rig and extended his hand. She took it, thinking he was not just irritatingly charming but a gentleman. When her foot touched the ground, Christine felt off balance. She steadied herself, not wanting to let Will know how addled she felt.

He released her and scooted around to the back of the carriage while the driver unloaded her luggage. When the large bag hit the road, Will pulled out the extension handle, grasped her carry-on and paid the driver.

Will led the way, and by the time she'd climbed the porch steps, he'd given a rap on the door, opened it and beamed his toying smile. "I live here."

Christine gave a nod, thinking he might live in the house, but her grandmother wasn't his. She hoped he remembered that. Hearing her grandmother's welcoming voice, she surged past him.

"Grandma," she said, sweeping into the cozy living room. She set her case on the carpet and opened her arms to her grandmother, noticing the droopiness on the right side of her face. Seeing her made the stroke seem so much more real. "You look good, Grandma Summers. As beautiful as ever."

Her grandmother shook her head, her hair now white, her body thinned by age and illness. "That's a wee bit of stretching the truth, Christine, but thank you. The truth is, you're as lovely as ever." Though her words were understandable, Christine noted a faint slur in her diction.

Christine ached seeing her grandmother's motionless left side. Her mind flew back to the first time she was old enough to remember a visit from her grandmother. Ella Summers had appeared to her as a tall, well-dressed woman with neat brown hair the color of wet sand and a loving smile. Today she still had a warm, but lopsided smile.

Choked by the comparison, Christine leaned down to embrace her. When she straightened, she glanced behind her, wondering what had happened to Will.

"I'm happy you're here," her grandmother said, "but I'm sorry it's because of my health. I feel so—"

"Just get better, Grandma. Don't worry about feeling guilty." Let me do that, Christine thought, as her grandmother's words heightened her feeling of negligence.

She slipped off her coat, but before she could dispose of it, a sound behind her caused Christine to turn.

Will stood with his shoulder braced against the living room doorjamb. He had removed his jacket, and she noticed his chestnut-colored sweater, nearly the color of his eyes. She pulled her attention away and focused on her grandmother.

"Now that I'm out of the hospital's rehab and you're here, I'll get better sooner," Ella said, trying to reach for her hand without success.

The picture cut through her. "Mom and Dad told me what happened, but I'd like to hear it from you." She draped her coat on the sofa, then sat in a chair closer to Grandma Summers.

Her grandmother's face pulled to a frown. "You know, Christine, my memory fails me when it comes to those first days. I can remember details of my childhood, but all I remember about my stroke is

Will found me and called nine-one-one. I'm not even sure if I remember that or if he told me about it."

"I can tell you what happened," Will said, stepping more deeply into the room.

Christine ignored his offer. She'd heard second-hand details. She wanted it from her grandmother. "I see the stroke affected your arm," Christine said, watching her grandmother's frustration grow when she'd tried to gesture.

"My left arm and leg. My leg doesn't cooperate, and I'm a little off balance." Discouragement sounded in her voice. "But I've made progress."

Christine patted her hand. "I'm so sorry."

"Where do you want her bags, Grandma Ella?"

Christine froze. Grandma Ella? At least, he could call her Grandma Summers. Even better, Mrs. Summers. She opened her mouth to comment.

"The room at the top of the stairs," her grandmother said.

Will winked and tipped an imaginary hat—cowboy hat in Christine's mind—before he headed up the staircase with her luggage.

"How long has he been here?" Christine asked, fighting the unexpected interest she had in him.

"Will's such a nice young man." Ella turned her gaze from the staircase to Christine. "He moved in at the beginning of the season last year in May. I decided I'd like to have someone around, and he's been a blessing. He's like a grandson."

A grandson? Christine weighed her grandmother's words, confounded by the unknown relationship. "Mom and Dad approved?"

"Certainly. They met him on visits before my stroke, but they became much better acquainted when they were here recently. You should come here more often, dear. You're out of the loop."

Christine could have chuckled at her grandmother's modern lingo, but guilt won out. An occasional trip to the island wouldn't hurt her.

"Will's been through so much with me. He's the one who called nine-one-one when he realized something was wrong. He saved my life."

She realized her grandmother had already told her that, but it was a point she couldn't forget. How could she dislike someone who had saved her grandmother's life?

Will's footsteps bounding down the stairs drew Christine's attention to the hallway. He whipped around the corner like a man who owned the place.

"How about some cocoa?" he asked. He gave her grandmother a questioning look.

"That would be nice," Ella said. "And you can bring in some of the cookies Mrs. Fields baked."

Christine chuckled.

"It's really Mrs. Fields, the neighbor. Not the franchise," Will said.

Christine watched him head into the next room, tired of his knowing everything. Right now, she really did feel out of the loop.

"Linda Fields has been helping me in the morning

since your mother left. Dressing myself is difficult. She does other things for me when Will's at work. She's been so kind."

Christine felt herself sinking lower in the chair. "You can't dress yourself?"

"I had therapy." She rubbed her temple with her right hand. "Occupational therapy, I think is what they call it. They showed me how to get dressed, but sometimes it's so frustrating. The therapist guarantees me I'll be as good as new again."

The vision of a neighbor helping her grandmother dress wavered in Christine's mind. She'd never dressed anyone, and the indignity for her grandmother seemed unbearable. "How long?"

"She's been coming in since your mother and father left."

"No. I meant how long before you'll be good as new?"

"It's up to the progress I make in my therapy. Judy, she's my therapist, only comes twice a week to see me, and I have to do the routine myself a couple times a day."

"Who helps you now?"

"Will or Linda, but Will's devoting too much time to me. He has his work."

Apparently he'd become her grandmother's superhero. "Mom'll be here soon, and you won't have to worry." Christine hated the feeling of inadequacy. She'd never nursed anyone. Apparently Will had. Will this. Will that.

With Will permeating her thoughts, another question struck her. "Who is he, Grandma Summers?"

Her eyes shifted with uncertainty. "He? You mean she. Judy's my therapist."

"No, I mean Will. Who is he?"

"He's a nice young man who needed a place to stay. I thought I told you."

"You did, but you mentioned he has a job. Is it here on the island?"

Her grandmother's eyes brightened. "Not just a job. He owns a store in town."

"Really?" So Will Whatever-His-Name was a businessman. "What kind of a store?" Hardware, she figured.

"He's an artist. Stained glass. It's so beautiful." Her grandmother's left arm twitched, and a look of despair washed over her. "I keep forgetting," she said, then gestured to the window with her right arm.

Christine looked to her left and saw a glass angel glinting in the growing sunlight. A rainbow decorated the carpet. She rose and wandered to the faceted design. Clear beveled glass shaped the figure about eight inches high. The angel clasped a vibrant floral bouquet, the only color in the lovely artwork.

"It's beautiful." The unbidden words slipped from Christine's mouth.

"Thank you."

His voice jarred her, and she turned toward Will, standing beside her grandmother, holding a tray.

He looked away and set it on the old chest her

grandmother used as a coffee table. "Here you go," he said, handing her grandmother a mug.

Christine grimaced as she watched Ella struggle to grasp the drink with one hand.

"Sorry," he said, retrieving the heavy crockery and pulling a straw from his pocket. "You've always been so independent it's hard to remember." His warm smile seemed attentive as he tore the paper wrapper from the straw and lowered it into her cocoa, then held it up for her to sip.

The chocolate aroma wafted in the air and reminded Christine of the years she was a child and her mother would make her hot chocolate in the evening as a lure toward bedtime.

Christine observed his attentiveness. He was not only a gentleman, but a gentle man. It seemed strange to her, and she couldn't help but question his motives.

When Will finished, he grasped another mug and offered it to Christine. The movement brought her back from her thoughts. "Thanks," she said, accepting the drink.

He pushed her coat to the far end of the sofa and sat. In silence, they sipped the chocolate, and Christine sensed each of them had sunk into their own thoughts. Hers asked questions about the man who sat across from her looking as if he belonged there while she knew she didn't. She belonged behind a desk at Creative Productions, where she generated unique promotion ideas for other companies' ad campaigns. The whole situation coursed through her like a bad case of stomach flu.

When she lifted her head, Will was eyeing her as if trying to read her thoughts. She turned to her grandmother. "Does your therapist fly in from St. Ignace?"

"She's from Vital Care located in St. Ignace," Will said, "but the nurse is on the island. She works at the Medical—"

"I was asking my grandmother," Christine said pointedly.

Ella shook her head. "Will knows the answers to all your questions, Christine."

"I know that, Grandma Summers, but—"

"He's been through the whole thing with me. He and Linda."

Christine lowered her gaze, reeling from her grandmother's subtle reprimand. She looked at Will. "I appreciate your help."

Ella's frown thawed. "Now that you're here, Christine, you can take over, and we can give Linda and Will a break."

Christine blinked. Bathe her grandmother? She worked in a think tank, not a bathtub. She paused while indignity coursed through her, not for herself but for her grandmother. How did she feel having to allow others to help her with tasks most people took for granted? "And Mom will be here soon," she said.

Ella lifted a warm gaze to Will. "Did I thank you for meeting Christine at the ferry dock?"

"No thanks necessary." He set down his mug and

rose. "I should get over to the studio. I have a big project I'm trying to finish."

Christine watched him stride toward the door, then pause and look back at them with his casual grin. A young John Wayne, she thought again.

He wasn't such a bad guy, she supposed, but he seemed way too familiar with her grandmother. He had to have an ulterior motive, and she felt determined to learn what it was.

Chapter Two

Will stood inside the small stable and placed the saddle pad on the horse. She whinnied and stamped her foot as if to say she wanted to go and wanted to go now. The action reminded him of Grandma Ella's granddaughter. She seemed to lack patience worse than the mare. And trust? She had less trust than a mother bird. He pictured her clinging to her carry-on at the ferry station, as if she had the crown jewels inside the little case.

He shifted to reach the saddle and lowered it on the horse's back, adjusting it on the pad to make sure it didn't rub the horse's withers. He gave Daisy a pat. Women. He didn't understand Christine at all, and rubbing? He must have rubbed her the wrong way. She didn't like him, and since the moment he'd met her, he'd trudged through his thoughts trying to imagine how he'd offended her. He must have, because she obviously had an attitude toward him with a capital *A*.

Still, she was prettier than the baroque glass he worked with in some of his stained-glass artwork. Like the glass, she had texture and lines—very pretty lines, he had to admit. Working with his art, he could lay out his pattern and select the most unique whorls and designs in the glass created by the melding colors, but with Ella's granddaughter, he had to deal with the whole of her. He couldn't lop off the parts that weren't as nice. Her attitude fell into that category.

Will bent down and buckled the cinch snug around the horse's belly. He checked the tightness, then adjusted the stirrups. When he rose, he paused a moment while Christine's image filled his mind. When he'd stood beside her near the taxi, he'd noticed she was only a couple inches shorter than his six feet, and she was as slender as a bead of solder. She was a work of art with a bad attitude.

He could still picture how her golden hair fell in waves and bounced against her shoulder. In the taxi, he couldn't help but admire her glowing skin, her wide-set eyes that studied him so intently. Hazel eyes, he guessed, as changeable as she seemed to be.

Will reached for the bridle and moved to the horse's left side. He placed his hand on the horse's forelock and pressed gently. Daisy lowered her head, and he grabbed the headstall, separated the mouthpiece from the reins and held it to the horse's mouth.

She opened it, and he slipped the bit gently inside, then pulled the headstall over the horse's ears. After he adjusted the chin strap, he gave Daisy's shoulders a pat.

"You're not bad-looking yourself, young lady." He tucked his hand into his pocket and pulled out a sugar cube. Daisy sensed it and lifted her head to nibble the sweet from the palm of his hand.

An unexpected thought came to him. What treat could he use to have Christine nibbling out of his palm? He wiped his hand on his jeans and gathered the reins. He leaned against the stall as once again his thoughts filtered through the morning's events. The woman had a message in her eye, warning that she didn't trust him and didn't want to try. He'd seen the same look of disdain on his father's face more often than he wanted to remember.

Will pulled his back away from the boards and led Daisy to the stable doorway, then shifted his focus toward the house.

He needed a plan. If he had to spend a week with this woman hovering beside Ella—her granddaughter no less—he had to find a way to get along with her. Daisy's sugar cube entered his mind again.

He kicked a stone with the toe of his boot and grunted. Get along? He got along fine with everyone else. The problem belonged to Christine.

Christine stepped into her guest bedroom and found her suitcase lying on the bed. Will had placed her small bag on a table beneath the window. Will again. He was like a woodpecker—irritating but intriguing.

Winter sunshine spread a spiderweb design on the table's wooden top. She wandered to the window and pushed back the lacy curtain. Will stood below just inside the stable doorway with a horse, saddled and ready to ride. Knowing he couldn't see her, she watched him staring into space as if his mind were faraway.

Seeing him with the horse, his hand on the reins, brought the same gentle cowboy to mind. She grinned at her imaginings. She'd daydreamed as a teenager but not as a woman with brains in her head.

A ragged sigh escaped her. What was it about the handsome man that she disliked? From the moment she'd laid eyes on him, he'd set her on edge, and it made no sense. She could only reason she was killing the messenger. He'd picked her up at the island ferry—a place she hadn't wanted to come.

She let the curtain drop and reminded herself the visit was only a week—eight days at the most. She had her laptop and her cell phone. Though it wouldn't be easy, business could be conducted that way, she hoped, for a short time.

She thought of her friend, Ellene, who'd had a similar gripe earlier in the year when she was stranded on Harsens Island in Lake St. Clair. She'd blown off Ellene's concern about island life, and now her friend was married to Connor and lived there. Amazing what love could do.

Love. She didn't really like the word. She'd been

bitten too badly to trust. At thirty-nine, marriage seemed an unlikely prospect.

Christine returned to the window and peeked out. Will had vanished from the doorway. She could see the horse's imprints in the mounting snow. Perhaps he'd gone to work. Good. He needn't worry about her grandmother any longer now that she was there. He could spend the whole day at his job.

Stained glass. A businessman and a creative type. He seemed too—she couldn't find the word—too lacka-daisical for a man who had to make a living running a business. Why hadn't he dropped her off and gone back to work instead of making them hot chocolate?

The delicate stained-glass angel filled her mind—a perfect gift for her grandmother, who'd always been a strong Christian. She could only deduce Will was a believer.

Sadness wove like tendrils into her conscience. She was a believer, but—but what? "Admit it," she mumbled. "The Bible says faith and actions work together, and faith is made complete by a person's good deeds."

Letting the thought fetter away, Christine slipped back the curtain again and scanned the yard. She had an empty feeling, thinking about her lack of compassion for others. It wasn't that she didn't care. She just didn't take the time.

She backed away and turned her attention to her luggage, slipped her pants into a drawer and her sweaters into another, then hung up a few items. Easy when she knew how to travel light. She pulled up her shoulders and drew in a lengthy breath.

"Be nice," she whispered to herself. The man had been kind to her grandmother. The next time she saw him she knew she should show her gratitude.

She left the bedroom and descended the staircase into the large foyer. She loved her grandmother's house with all the nooks and crannies of an elegant Victorian home. So many lovely homes had been built on the island in the late 1800s.

The first floor greeted her with silence. She paused to listen. Still hearing nothing, she crossed the tiles to the living room doorway and saw her grandmother seated where she'd left her, her head resting against the wing of the chair. Her eyes were closed, and her chest rose and fell in an easy rhythm.

She studied her grandmother's face a moment, the classic lines—a well-sculpted nose, wide-set eyes as green as a new leaf, a full mouth that always curved upward into a pleasant grin, her mother's features in her grandmother's face.

Christine smiled at her grandmother's quiet beauty. Even though the stroke had left its mark, she felt confident her grandmother would get well.

"Nice smile."

Christine's heart jolted, and she swung toward the window seat that looked out to the garden. She poked her index finger into her chest. "Me?" she whispered, not wanting to wake her grandmother.

He gave a quiet chuckle and tilted his head toward the sleeping form. "She's not smiling so it must be you." His voice was hushed, and he glanced toward her grandmother as if to make sure he hadn't awakened her.

Christine tiptoed across the carpet and settled onto the next window seat. "Why are you sitting in here?"

"Waiting for you."

"Me?"

Will tilted his head. "She's sleeping so I'm not—"

"Waiting for her, I know." The man confounded her. "Why are you waiting, and where's your horse?"

His eyebrows raised, and she realized she'd given herself away.

"You were watching me?"

"No. I happened to look out the window."

He flashed her a teasing smile. "Daisy's tied up outside ready to go. I thought you might need something in town."

She frowned, looking for his motive.

Will rose, his grin fading to match her scowl. "I'm trying to be nice. I want you to feel welcome."

"I always feel welcome at my grandmother's."

"But I've never seen you here in the past year and a half. Maybe since you've visited last, she's moved the silverware to a different drawer."

His barb added another notch to her guilt. "I can find the silverware. Thank you."

He shook his head and strutted to the doorway. "Have a nice day."

"You too," she said, thinking hers would be nicer with him gone, but the thought gave her a kick. She was being so unfair. Jealousy? Was that it? Was she being that childish about ownership of her grandmother? The idea hounded her as she hurried from the room.

"Will," she called, having distanced herself from the living room doorway. She headed in the direction she suspected he'd gone. "Will."

He didn't respond, and she dropped her arms to her sides.

"You called?"

Her neck jerked upward, and she looked at him near the back hallway. Now facing him, her apology knotted in her throat. "Look, I'm—I'm sorry. It's not your fault that I'm here. It's no one's fault. My parents planned their trip, and my grandmother didn't know she was having a stroke. I—" She stopped not knowing what else to say.

He looked at her questioningly. "It's okay. Sometimes things happen that we don't expect, and it's difficult to adjust plans. My parents like planning everything to the letter. My father wishes I would, but I don't. As he would say in the words of Shakespeare, 'Ay, there's the rub.'"

"You're quoting Shakespeare?"

He laughed, and the look in his eyes unsettled her. His rich smile reflected in the sparkling blue of his iris. "Like everyone, I took English lit at university."

"You were a college man?"

His smile faded. She studied him, curious why her question had triggered the negative look.

He seemed to regroup. "For nearly three years."

No degree? "What was your major? Art?" she asked.

"Business."

Business. She drew back, startled by the new information. "So where does the art come in?"

His eyes drifted, and she could see he was uncomfortable with the probing.

"I left U of M and went to Creative Studies in Detroit, then to Carnegie Mellon in Pittsburgh."

Now that really knocked her off guard. "I'm impressed."

"Don't be," he said.

His comment was so abrupt Christine didn't understand what happened. "I don't mean to keep you."

"I'm on my way." He took a step backward. "Drop by the studio sometime."

"If I have time. My grandmother's my priority."

He gave a quick nod and headed out the front door. She followed and watched him through the Victorian glass window. He put his foot into the stirrup, flung his trim leg over the saddle and snapped the reins. The horse took off at a good gait and, before long, he'd vanished around the bend.

She let out a sigh. The conversation had been strange. Strange and strained. Something bothered Will, and she wondered if her grandmother knew his problem.

With her grandmother in mind, Christine returned to the living room, and when she came through the doorway, her grandmother opened her eyes. "I guess I caught a little catnap."

"Naps are good for you. I unpacked and talked with Will a few minutes."

Her grandmother straightened. "Why don't you like Will, Christine?"

"Why don't I what?"

"I can see you don't like Will, and I can't understand why. I'm sure Will sees it too."

"I apologized to him before he left. I know I was a little abrupt."

"But why, dear?"

Christine wandered deeper into the room and sank into a nearby chair. "I—I keep thinking he must have an ulterior motive."

"Will? He's as gentle as a lamb and so kindhearted."

She ached watching her grandmother try to gesture again. "But why is he so thoughtful? You're his landlady."

Her grandmother straightened in the chair. "Because he follows God's Word. He clothes himself with compassion and kindness. You're a Christian. You should understand that."

"I—" She felt her heel tapping against the carpet and tried to stop herself before her grandmother noticed. Christine knew she would disappoint her if she admitted her faith had paled from the actions of her youth.

"What motive do you think he has?" Her grand-mother's sentence came out disjointed.

"I don't know." She wanted to end the direction of the conversation. "I just think a mature male would have better things to do than to be a nursemaid to—"

"An old lady."

Christine flinched. "I didn't mean it that way, Grandma." She wished she could just keep her mouth shut. Where was the tact she used in the business world?

"I know." Her vivid green eyes captured Christine's. Christine could barely look in her eyes. "I'm—"

"You're a career woman," Ella said. "You make important deals and enjoy success. I'm proud of you, but you can also be kind and still be successful. God says, there will be a time for every activity, a time for every deed. In fact, success is even greater when it's done with a humble heart and a desire to please the Lord."

Christine fought her tears. She felt like a child being chastised by her parents for misbehaving, but this was Grandma Summers, and grandmothers were supposed to be supportive and forgiving.

Yet her grandmother was right. Christine had been unpleasant, but she'd thought she'd had good reason. "I did apologize."

"I know. You told me." She eased back and didn't say any more.

Christine's mind slid back to that moment. "What's in the back hall off the foyer? Will came from that way."

"It's the back entry. He can come from the apartment that way or leave to go outside. I can lock that door, but it's been convenient for me."

"Is that how he found you after you had the stroke?"

"It was. He came in one morning to see if I wanted anything from the store in town. He found me confused and weak. At least that's what he tells me. I tried to walk and couldn't. That's when he called for help. Fast thinking."

"I'm glad he was here," Christine said, and meant every word. She rose and kissed her grandmother's cheek. "So what can I do for you? Can I help you with your therapy?"

She glanced around the room and noticed dust on the table. "I can dust and run the vacuum." She crossed the room and gathered shoes and a jacket from the floor. "What should I do with these?"

The shoes were definitely not her grandmother's. They were men's shoes, and so was the jacket. "Will's?"

Her grandmother chuckled. "He drops his belongings like a teenager, but I don't mind. It's nice to have someone here."

"Well, he shouldn't cause you extra work. He has his own home. I'll talk to him."

Her grandmother shook her head. "Sometimes Will forgets. Don't worry about cleaning. Will pitches in, and I should really hire a cleaning lady for a while."

"Mom will be here. She won't want a cleaning lady.

You know Mom. You do it her way or no way." She chuckled, then realized she'd almost described herself.

Her grandmother gave a nod, then gestured toward a table with a toss of her head. "See that little ball? Would you hand it to me? I'm supposed to squeeze it off and on during the day to strengthen my muscles."

Christine handed her the ball and had turned to discard Will's belongings when the telephone rang. "I'll get it." She headed toward the small secretary and picked up the receiver. "Summers residence."

When she heard her father's voice, her spirit lifted. "Daddy, where are you?"

She covered the mouthpiece and turned to her grandmother. "They're in Jamaica. I can hear the steel drum band." Christine longed to be on some exotic island with sunshine and balmy breezes. "Are you having fun?"

"A great time. Fantastic." His voice boomed.

"I'm really happy for you, Dad."

"How's Grandma? And be honest, Christine."

"Grandma's fine." She couldn't believe he told her to be honest. "Really. We're doing okay, and you'll be here soon. We'll see you on Monday, right?"

Her heart sank a little with his answer.

"Okay, Wednesday will work. I can leave on the afternoon ferry if you're early enough. Love you both."

She hung up and faced her grandmother. "It's eighty-five degrees there."

"I'm sure they're having a wonderful time," she said, her eyes searching Christine's.

Guilt blanketed her again. She needed to fix her attitude. The problem was timing. Timing? Face it, she thought, no time was ever good for Christine. She liked to plan her course and sail away with no waves, but things didn't always happen the way she wanted. She needed to learn to roll with the tide. Will's comment about things not always going as planned echoed in her thoughts.

"I'd like to go to church tomorrow," Ella said. "It's difficult, but I have the wheelchair. Would you like to go?"

"Church?" She stood in the middle of the room and looked out the wide front window and across the porch to the splotches of white and tried to envision what good a wheelchair would do in the snow. "But how—"

"Will can handle it. We'll get a taxi. It's just a short ride down Fort Hill."

Christine stopped herself from rolling her eyes. Will again. "Is it worth the trouble, Grandma?"

"Worth it? What has more worth than spending time with the Lord?"

She closed her mouth before she put her foot in it again. "I meant it's so difficult for you."

"My therapist said I should try to get out. I've been too embarrassed to have anyone see me so useless. My face is drooping. I can see that in the mirror."

Christine knelt beside her grandmother. "You're not useless. I'm sorry I said anything. I—"

Her grandmother patted her arm with a weak hand. "You didn't make me feel that way, Christine. I'm just…" She paused and looked at her unaccommodating fingers. "Did I ever tell you about when I was a girl?"

Christine figured she'd heard every youthful tale of her grandmother's, but she'd already hurt her feelings enough. "I don't know, Grandma."

Ella gave her a tender look and leaned back in her chair. "When I was a girl, my mother sent all of us to Bible school during the summer. It was like a summer camp but at the church. We learned so much about compassion and giving to others. We memorized Bible verses. One of my favorites was that whatever you do, whether in word or deed, do it all in the name of the Lord Jesus. Even as a girl, I realized that our deeds reflect our faith."

Christine recalled thinking that same thing earlier that day, and she wondered if the Lord was pounding a lesson into her head. "I know, Grandma, but—"

"No buts. We had a project one year at the Bible camp. We visited a hospital to bring little gifts we made to some of the elderly patients. I saw a woman there unable to use her limbs. At the time I didn't know anything about strokes, but I'm sure that's what it was. She couldn't speak well, either. That very day I promised the Lord I would always be kind to people in need. So being useless myself makes it doubly hard because of the promise I made to God."

How could she argue with her grandmother's way

of looking at her vow. Christine figured God was the one who had allowed her grandmother to have a stroke. He knew she couldn't continue to be helpful, so He'd have to forgive her breaking her vow. But she couldn't verbalize that to her grandmother.

"Then, I think, it's most important that you get better. Right, Grandma?"

"Right," she said, a gentle look in her eyes. "And that's why I want to go to church."

"Then you and I will go to church," Christine said.

"You and me and Will."

Christine managed to smile. "You and me and Will."

Chapter Three

"There, that wasn't so bad." Will stomped the snow from his shoes on the porch mat. Today when he'd awakened, he was surprised to see a heavy snow had fallen while he'd slept, leaving the island shrouded in white.

He wheeled Grandma Ella through the front door to the middle of the foyer. "Let me take your coat."

"I can get her coat," Christine said, bustling toward him.

He shrugged. "It's all yours." He tried to figure out the big deal. Either one of them could help her. It wasn't like a jump ball in a basketball game.

Christine hung her grandmother's coat in the foyer closet, then hung up her own and closed the door without a glance his way.

Will shook his head and passed her, removed his wet shoes and left them by the living room archway, not wanting to dirty Ella's carpet. He headed across the carpet, shrugged off his jacket and hung it on a chair, then settled on the sofa.

Yesterday's newspaper lay on the floor. Will lifted it to his lap and swung his feet around to spread out on the cushions. Though he tried to focus on the first page, his attention had shifted over the top of the paper toward the foyer.

Christine came through the doorway pushing Ella's wheelchair. He really wished Grandma Ella would get out of the thing. She needed to get her legs working and strengthen the muscles. That would alleviate her unsteadiness. He'd encouraged her to use the walker, but she said she felt like an old lady.

Christine turned his way, and her expression let him know she wasn't pleased to see him sprawling on the sofa.

Will dropped the paper onto the floor and swung his feet to the carpet. "Sorry. Usually on Sundays, I keep Grandma Ella company for a while. Am I taking up too much space?"

A pink tinge lit Christine's cheeks. "No." She sank onto the chair with a sigh. "Not at all."

"What's wrong, dear?" her grandmother asked.

"Nothing."

"You look unhappy."

"Really. I'm fine."

A look of uneasiness filled her face, and she gave Will a smile that looked a little forced to him.

She studied her fingernails for a moment. "I need

to go into town. I should have thought of it while we were there for church. I noticed at breakfast we need a few things from the grocery store."

Will glanced at his watch. "It's Sunday. The store's just about to open. I'll take you," he said. "I need to drop by the studio anyway and pick up some paperwork I forgot to bring home."

"You have a tandem bike, or am I supposed to ride with you on the horse?" As the words left her, she concocted another grin.

The look on her face made him laugh. "No, but that's a good idea. Daisy would love to go for a good run this morning. She leaves for the mainland tomorrow."

Christine looked surprised "Leaves?"

He loved to confound her. "Once the heavy snow begins, Daisy is stabled at a farm on the mainland. Only the horses used for taxis and drays stick around here for the winter."

Christine gave him a look. "The horses are smarter than people, I think."

He chuckled, but he got her point. He jumped up and headed for the doorway. "We'll take my sled… or you can ride your grandmother's."

"Sled?"

He laughed aloud this time. "Snowmobile."

"You want me to drive myself? I don't know a thing about snowmobiles."

"One day I'll give you a lesson then."

"Yes," Grandma Ella said, "that's a good idea."

Christine held up her hand in protest. "I'm leaving next week. Save the lesson for my mom." She chuckled.

Will enjoyed her unexpected good humor and wished he could always see that side. "You can ride with me. I'd like you to see my studio anyway."

"You'll enjoy seeing the shop," her grandmother agreed.

She paused a moment, then said, "Okay."

Will glanced back to make sure he had heard her correctly. No argument?

"Who can I call to stay with you, Grandma Summers?" Christine asked.

Her grandmother waved her away. "I'm not a baby. I can stay by myself for an hour. Put the portable phone next to me, and set my walker here. I'll use it if I need to get up."

"We won't be gone long," Will assured Christine, then turned to Grandma Ella, "and we can check on you, okay?"

"I'll be fine. You can't tie an old horse down for long."

Christine chuckled. "If you were a horse, Will would be shipping you over to St. Ignace."

Will gave her a high five, and to his amazement, she responded and took a step backward toward the foyer.

"I'll change and make a list," she said.

"Keep it short," Will said. "We go to the mainland for the bulk of the groceries."

Christine stopped and motioned toward the window. "But what about when—"

"No ferry service? Then supplies are flown in." He enjoyed teaching this strong-willed woman about island life.

She arched a neatly trimmed brow. "As I said, island living isn't very convenient, is it?"

"No, but then if you're looking for convenience you don't live on an island."

Christine gave him a see-I-told-you-so look.

Will didn't bother to comment. "I'll change and be ready in a minute. And remember, we're not going back if you forget anything."

She looked as if she wanted to say something but didn't.

Christine stood outside the small barn, eyeing Will's snowmobile and trying to imagine herself seated on it. She'd surprised herself by agreeing to ride the thing, but she needed to get around, and walking down and up hills to town in snow appealed to her even less than riding with Will.

She felt like the Abominable Snowman, with a sweatshirt and down jacket over her sweater. She could barely move. With two pairs of socks under the tall boots she had borrowed from her grandmother—already a little tight—she tromped through the snow like Frosty on a bad day.

"Are you warm enough?" Will asked.

"I hope so." She could only deduce that his silly

expression was lighthearted sarcasm. She shifted her attention to the snowmobile. "You want me to get on this thing?"

Will lifted his hand. "Hang on a minute." He walked back into the stable and came out carrying two helmets. "You're not going anywhere without this."

He tossed her one, and she nearly dropped it. "I'm supposed to wear this?"

"You're not only supposed to—you will. It's for your safety. No one gets on my sled without one."

Sled? She pictured the little red sled from her childhood, then eyed the monstrosity he was telling her to get on. She gazed at the helmet and then at him. How much danger was she in?

"Put it on," he said, slipping some kind of hood over his head.

"What's that?"

"A smock. You'll have to get one." He slid the helmet onto his head and attached the strap.

She followed what he'd done, attached the strap and felt as if she had a cooking pot on her head with a large shield over her face. "I look stupid."

"You don't look stupid," he said, accentuating the word "look."

"I hear a *but* in that statement."

"I'm not going there," he said, a teasing smile growing on his face.

Will looked amazingly handsome, his broad shoulders accentuated beneath his sledding jacket.

Below the helmet, his eyes sparkled when he looked at her. "Okay, Bigfoot, can you climb on?"

He made her laugh. She liked that but not his I-know-more-about-island-life-than-you-do attitude. Earlier she'd tried to cover her amusement with sarcasm, but lately he had a cute way to get back at her. She felt like a kid again, rather than the dignified woman she'd considered herself to be.

She'd studied Will, weighing his boyish charm and easy manner, and had pondered how old he might be. She'd wanted to know, but she knew good manners, and one couldn't blatantly ask. She'd be irked if he asked her.

Christine straddled the vehicle as best she could, then plopped onto the seat, scooting back as far as she could to make room for him. She felt her cell phone press against her leg. She'd tucked it in her pocket.

He waited for her to get settled, then slipped in front of her. "I made it. You're not as fat as you look."

She gave him a jab. "I feel undignified enough. Don't add to it."

"Dignity is nothing without a sense of humor."

"I don't mind laughing *with* someone, but I don't want to be laughed *at* by someone," she said.

"Then next time, you'll have to leave about half that garb at home." He grinned. "You need a bib."

"A bib? I'm not eating lobster."

"Snow pants, to you," he said, chuckling. "You'll get used to it, and if I were a betting man, I'd wager you'll get to love the island even in winter."

"You're on," she said. "If I love it here, I owe you something big. A seven-course dinner or—" She faltered, realizing she was having a good time.

"I'll make that decision when I collect," he said with a wink over his shoulder. "Now keep your feet on the foot board." He pulled the cord and started the engine. He revved the motor to warm it, sending another grin with each vroom-vroom sound. "Ready?"

"Absolutely," she said, then jolted backward when the sled shot forward. She let out a squeal and clung to him, her arms wrapped around his waist, praying her feet were glued to the footrest.

He paused at the end of the driveway. "Lean with me on the turns," he called over his shoulder.

She nodded, and he rolled forward, then made a right toward Custer Road.

Above the roar of the engine, he hollered back his usual witty comments, his youthful spirit evident as they soared across the snow. Youthful, yet he had depth, too, Christine had noticed. She saw the heavy thoughts in his eyes. She watched the tenderness he had for her grandmother, and Christine couldn't help but notice how he studied her. She didn't think he'd figured her out yet, but he would.

The wind whipped past, and Christine clung to Will's body for warmth and security. A chill rolled down her back despite her heavy clothing, or wasn't it the wind at all? She'd never done anything quite so daring, and perhaps it was only the adventure that took her breath away and sent excitement prickling up her spine.

Will seemed to be in his element—relaxed and carefree. She wished she could be more like him, more easygoing, and definitely more trusting.

The snow-burdened trees shimmered in the muted winter sun, and occasionally the clouded sky opened to let a bright ray stream down to earth and drop sequins in the snow. She closed her eyes from the glitter.

"Hang on," Will called.

Her heart rose to her throat as they made a curve past the governor's house and flew down Fort Hill and the whitewashed buildings flashed past her. She clung to him even tighter, enjoying the unfamiliar feeling of holding a man in her arms.

Instead of heading to Main Street, Will slowed and turned onto Market Street. They shot past the medical center and post office. Along the way, the quaint shops and homey bed-and-breakfasts lined the road, adorned with green-and-red wreaths and garland announcing Christmas. Finally he decelerated and pulled to the curb. "Here we are."

She looked at the store beside her. The window held displays of magnificent stained-glass windows, and sun catchers in all shapes and sizes hung from the French panes. The brilliant colors glinted in the afternoon rays.

The quiet street seemed so different from the hustle and bustle she recalled from the summer afternoons when tourists packed the streets—*fudgies,* the residents called them, because most visitors left the island with boxes of homemade fudge purchased in the famous island fudge shops.

Will climbed from the sled and extended his hand. Christine looked at it and at her feet adhered to the running board, her body cramped from clinging to Will's waist as they flew across the unblemished snow. "I'm not sure I can move."

He pulled off his helmet, his grin as wide as the Mackinac Bridge, and shook his head. "Let me help."

She gave him her hand and dismounted, her knees trembling from the bumpy vibration of the sled. "I need to get my land legs."

He drew closer, balancing her in his arms. "You'll get used to it."

But could she ever become used to being held in a wonderful man's arms? The thought rushed down her limbs, and, embarrassed, Christine stepped away and pulled off her helmet.

Will took it from her and hung it with his on the handlebars.

For a moment, Christine felt overwhelmed by the newness of her experiences, but she had to admit she felt exhilarated. The fresh air, the wind nipping at her cheeks, the unspoiled beauty of the landscape, the feel of Will's arms—it all had painted a memory in her mind and on her senses.

She drew in another breath, filling her lungs with pure air. "It smells wonderful."

"The cold freezes the horse dung."

His surprising comment made her laugh. "That's very romantic." As the word left her, she tried to stop it, but it was too late. Why would she say *romantic* to a man she barely knew and probably would never see again once she returned home?

"Thanks," he said. "I'm glad I can make a good impression on someone in this world."

Though he smiled, Christine sensed an undertone in his voice. She eyed him, but he didn't give a hint of what he had meant and she didn't know him well enough to pry, although she was tempted.

Will pulled a ring of keys from his pocket and headed for the door while Christine moved closer to the shop window to take a better look at his artwork. She saw the name on the window, Sea of Glass. She'd heard that phrase before.

Her mind shifted back to Will's behavior. He was hiding something or… Maybe he was more like she was than she'd thought. Now that she'd gotten through her own murky days as a naive businesswoman, she had gained confidence and had also developed a deep curiosity to look more deeply into people.

People said much more below the surface than their words expressed. Subliminal messages were important in the advertising business. She needed curiosity to sense what the company really wanted to convey in their ads, and then needed it again to express the underlying message to the consumer. If Will was playing games, he didn't know with whom he was messing.

Will pushed open the door, and a bell tinkled,

catching her attention. Christine followed him inside, feeling the warmth of the building and the varied aromas of raw wood, dust and all the products that went into stained-glass art. She knew nothing about it, but she was awed by what she saw.

"This is beautiful, Will." She paused beneath a large window hanging from the ceiling. A rich tapestry of colors created a pastoral scene with flowers, a river, sun and shade—multiple hues of greens and blues. "How do you do this? It's amazing."

"Very carefully," he said, the playful tone returning to his voice.

Her admiration rose as she turned in a circle to view the magnificent pieces of glass designs that adorned the store. "You learned to do this in college?"

He shrugged. "It's like anything. You learn techniques, and then you let your creativity take flight. You must do something creative in your own work—maybe something different than me, but still unique and your own style."

She searched his face, surprised at the matter-of-fact way he discussed his art. Something bothered him. "I suppose I do, but it's very different."

He stood a moment in silence. "Why is it different?"

"In advertising, I create ads and promotional campaigns for clients."

"That's creative." He gave one of his sun catchers a poke. "It's the same. You didn't learn everything in college."

"That's very true." She thought of all the mistakes

she'd made and her feeble attempts to cover them. "I work with a team. I can always blame them for my errors in judgment. You can't."

"No, but what's the difference. You know you made the mistake, the same as I do."

His comment left her flailing. He'd pinpointed an important issue that hit too close to home. No matter what she had done wrong, she knew about it herself—and so did God.

She looked a Will's expectant face, his eyes searching hers as if filled with questions he didn't have the nerve to ask. Something about him was endearing. "I'm really impressed." She made a sweeping gesture around the store, seeing wooden crates filled with gigantic pieces of marvelous glass in many colors and textures.

"I figured you'd like some of my things."

"Some? Everything is unique."

His questioning look faded, and a grin replaced it. "Then come into my back room and see some more of my work."

Will winked, then smiled at her over his shoulder.

Christine had to admit he had a wonderful smile that seemed contagious. She wanted to grin back, but she wasn't planning to let him know she found him attractive.

He passed through the doorway. "This is my studio where I make all of these things."

She followed him through the door and paused. She'd seen the supplies he sold in the front of the store, but in the back she surveyed worktables laden with projects and crates with a mixture of glass nearby.

"Where did you get the name for the shop—Sea of Glass?"

He turned to face her. "It's in the Bible. Revelations. Those who were victorious over Satan stood beside the sea of glass as clear as crystal." He gestured toward the lake. "The studio's only a couple blocks from the water. I thought it was fitting."

"It is. I like it."

"Glass is like people," he said, holding up a piece. "If you just glance at it, you see one thing, but if you really look inside—" he held it toward the light "—you see all kinds of nuances and textures."

She ran her finger over the swirled design, wondering what he'd seen inside her. "What kind of glass is this?"

"Baroque." He slid the large piece back into the rack, then selected another. "This is water glass."

Christine looked at the texture appearing like raindrops.

"And this is a smooth ripple. Here's an opal glass, bull's-eye, English muffle and cathedral glass."

"You've lost me."

He lowered the glass and then stepped closer and tousled her already messed hair. "No, I haven't. You're right here. See." He stepped closer and gave her a quick hug.

The embrace surprised yet pleased her. Will looked different in the studio, as if he were in control of his life. She saw confidence, and a look on his face that intrigued her—pride and a kind of wholeness. She wished she felt that way.

"You love this work," she said. "I can see it on your face."

"I do. It's like cheating. I earn a living doing something that I have to do because I can't help myself."

"That's not cheating. It's finding the right job."

He patted a stool beside the tall raw-wood table. "Sit here."

She slid onto the stool, and he leaned his hip against the table.

"Have you found the right career?" he asked.

"I like to think so. When we do a good job and make the client happy, I can sit back and see the result of my work. It feels good."

"That's what counts." He shifted away, but his response left her questioning her own decisions. She saw a specific difference between Will's attitude toward his work and hers.

"Would you like to see how I do any of these things?" He motioned toward the projects scattered around the room.

"I'd love to, but I think we'd better get going. I'm nervous about leaving my grandmother too long."

He nodded, then reached beneath his worktable and pulled out a large folded paper. "A pattern I'm designing. I'll show you back at the house."

"I'd like that," she said. "Let's go. We still have to stop at the grocery store."

As the words left her, her cell phone played its familiar tune. She dug into her pocket, curious yet concerned. "I left the number with Grandma. I hope she's okay." She stared at it, afraid to answer.

"You'll know, if you answer that thing."

The melody stopped when she hit the green button. "Hello," she said, expecting to hear her grandmother's voice, but who she heard instead gave her a start. "Dad. Where are you?"

She heard the upset in his voice, and she listened as her pulse pounded in her temple.

"You're in Florida? Why?"

Her stomach tightened as her world crumpled. She turned her head toward Will, unable to believe what she'd just heard.

She closed her eyes, then opened them again. "My mother fell and broke her hip, jogging."

Chapter Four

Christine watched Will's jaw drop. "Your mother broke her hip jogging? Where?"

"On the ship's promenade deck." She crumpled back onto the stool. "I can't believe this. This is a bad dream."

Will rose and rested his hand on her back. His warmth rushed through her. "I'm sure she'll be fine. She's in Florida, you said. Don't worry about—"

"Not that. I'm stuck here, Will. Don't you understand? I need to get back to my job. I thought I'd be home in a few days. Now what?"

She could see he'd been taken aback. His dark eyes flashed with disbelief, and she tried to recover from his look. "Naturally I'm concerned about my mother, but like you said, she'll be okay. I just wasn't planning on something like this happening."

"We don't plan for bad things to happen, Christine, but they do."

She stared at him, wanting to say something, to explain, to have someone understand her stress, but she knew it was useless. Will didn't know her at all. He had no idea about her work or how hard it was to stay at the top. "I'll figure out something."

Will pulled his hand away, leaving a cold spot where warmth had been. Her mood felt the same. Without expecting it, she'd enjoyed the outing and new experience of the snowmobile, but now the fun had faded.

She rose from the stool. "We'd better get moving. I'm sure my grandmother is upset about this, too. Daddy called there first. I know Grandma's fine, but she'll be worried about me."

"That's just like your grandmother," Will said, walking ahead of her and snapping off the lights. He tucked the folded paper inside his jacket and waited at the door for her, his hand on the knob.

Outside, the wind seemed colder than it had felt earlier. Christine sank onto the sled, scooted back and waited for Will to climb on and help block the bitter air. Tears filled her eyes, and she brushed them away with her gloves. She felt sorry for herself, and she hated the feeling. *Lord, I'm trying to make this a go. I want to be thoughtful and compassionate, but this isn't helping.*

God's voice didn't fill her head with an answer. The only sound she heard was the rev of the engine as they sped away. She wrapped her arms around Will's trim waist, his broad shoulders blocking the wind—just as he seemed to want to protect her from her problems.

"Hang on," he called.

That's what she needed to do—hang on. But to what?

When Will stopped outside Doud's Mercantile, Christine saw a smart-looking snowmobile on display. "They sell sleds at the grocery store?"

Will grinned. "No. It's for the Christmas Bazaar the first weekend in December. They hold a fund-raiser, and the prize is this sweet-looking baby right here." He gave the sled a pat. "It's the best of its line."

"It's really nice. Tell me what to do, and I'll donate to the fund-raiser, but I never win prizes. If I do, I'll give the sled to you."

Will gave her shoulder a squeeze.

Christine flew through the grocery store, paid for the purchases, donated to the fund-raiser, then headed back to her grandmother's in silence, her mind having slipped back to her problem.

The fun had vanished from the trip as quickly as the sun had hidden behind the heavy clouds and refused to come out. The cold penetrated her body, as did her dismay, and she felt icy to the bone.

Will put away the sled while Christine hurried into the house. She dropped her packages on the kitchen counter, then rushed toward the living room while she pulled off her coat. When she came through the doorway, her grandmother's concerned eyes lifted to hers.

Christine dropped her coat on a chair and put her

arms around her grandmother's shoulders. "What a predicament, Grandma Summers. Poor Mom."

Ella's face reflected her concern, but her demeanor negated the look. "I'll manage, dear, but tell me what happened. Your father only told me your mother had broken her hip, of all things."

Christine shared the story that her father had told her. "It was the wind, I guess. He said the prow of the ship has a powerful wind. Mom lost her balance and fell."

"But he said they were in Florida," Ella said.

"Yes, they airlifted her there. They have a doctor on board, but they can't do surgery like that on the ship."

Her grandmother shook her head. "How long before—"

"Daddy didn't know." The back door banged closed, and Christine lifted her head. "Mom'll need surgery and rehab. It'll be weeks."

"Many weeks, I'd guess," Will said from the doorway. He strutted in and plopped into a chair. "Looks like you'll need a snowmobile lesson after all."

Christine didn't like the faint grin he tried to hide without success.

"Don't jump to conclusions," she said. "I have to go back to work. Somehow." She felt the air leave her lungs.

He pinched his thumb and index finger and slid them across his mouth. "Zip."

"Zip?"

"I've zipped my mouth shut."

Good, she thought, then had second thoughts. He

was a nice guy—an appealing man—but she certainly didn't want to hear his jokes about her predicament.

She turned back to her grandmother. "Don't worry. I'll see you have good care. I'm sure you'll get better and better each day."

Christine wondered if she was trying to convince herself of that even more than her grandmother. Good care could come from a professional. Christine's mind began to snap with ideas.

Her grandmother's expression broke her heart. "I know," she said, "but this is difficult for you all the way around."

"I'd better get dinner," Christine said, rising and motioning toward the kitchen. "I left the groceries on the counter." Anxious to think by herself, she didn't wait for a response but hurried into the kitchen.

She stood inside the doorway, taking in the tall painted cabinets and tiled countertops. She shifted to the groceries and pulled items from the shopping bags, totally oblivious to what she'd planned to make her grandmother for Sunday dinner.

As she clung to the refrigerator, Christine's mind raced. Tomorrow she had work to do. First she needed to alert her boss of the complication, with a guarantee she would be back on the job soon. Next she needed to let her parents know she couldn't stay. How could she break that news to her father, who was already under so much stress and worry?

"Can I help?"

Christine spun around to face Will. So much for

time to think. His gentle look eased through her senses. "No thanks. I have things under control."

"You don't look like it," he said, closing the distance and taking a box of cereal from her hands. "Cereal goes in the cabinet." He opened the door and looked at her over his shoulder. "Milk goes in the refrigerator."

He lifted the milk from the cabinet and carried it back to her, leaned past her, and set the carton on the shelf. Then he moved her aside and closed the door. "Perhaps you'd better sit for a minute and get a grip."

She studied him, wanting to make some kind of retort but had nothing in her head to say. Milk in the cabinet and cereal in the refrigerator did nothing to convince him of her solid state of mind.

Christine did as he said and sank onto a kitchen chair, putting her face in her hands. She rubbed her eyes, willing herself not to cry. She'd figured she could handle the seven or eight days from her work, but now?

Will's warm hand rested on her shoulder again and gave her taut muscles a squeeze. "It'll be all right. Things will work out the way God planned them."

She looked at his face, filled with sincerity. "But what about what I planned? I have a job and I have to answer to someone. I'm not like you. I'm not my own boss. I work with a team. I'm responsible for what I do." She slapped her hand against the table. "I have clients."

"Me, too," he said, his voice as calm as a mother's reassurance.

She lifted her head and looked at him. "What clients?"

"I do special orders. I set deadlines, and I keep them. I'm proud of my work, and I do well. And I have a boss."

"You do? I thought you owned the business."

"I do," he said, using his thumbs to massage away the tension from her shoulders. "My big boss is the Lord. Whatever I do I answer to Him."

"It's not the same," she said, uneasy with his half-joking comments.

Will pulled his hand away and captured her chin and lifted it. "I'm not kidding with you. I answer to the Lord, and that's much more powerful than answering to the head of a corporation. One situation deals with a lifetime, the other eternity."

Christine pulled her chin away. "I know that, but I can't be lighthearted about my career." She turned her head.

"Neither can I. I've given up a lot for it. More than I should have."

He'd piqued her curiosity, and she turned back to look at him. "What does that mean?"

Will pursed his lips and shook his head. "That's my problem. You have enough of your own."

She didn't want to deal with her own. Christine wanted the problems to go away, to fade with the evening sun. She drew in a breath and managed to rise. "It's dinnertime."

"I know. I'm hungry. Let me help."

She gave him a quick look. "Don't you have your own kitchen?"

"A small one. Haven't you ever seen my apartment?"

She ignored his question. "I'm making dinner for my grandmother."

"I pay room and *board*," he said. "That means your grandmother cooks for me when she's well."

Room and board. The phrase sank in. He paid her grandmother for his food. She thought he'd eaten there last night because her grandmother had invited him. She gathered her thoughts, ashamed of her reaction to his attempt to be kind. "Okay, you can help. Do you know how to make a salad?"

"Sure. I make a great salad, but—" He hesitated, a deep frown on his face. "I think I'll go out for a while. Don't worry about me for dinner."

Christine opened her mouth to apologize, but he'd already shot from the room. She heard the back door bang closed, and she stood there staring at an empty room and feeling even more empty inside.

Will pushed the burger around on his plate and stared out the window of the Mustang Lounge. The view was nothing spectacular, no shoreline, just small shops across the street and new flakes drifting down to whiten the graying ground from the day's traffic.

Will had tried to understand Christine's attitude. She'd been disappointed by her father's news, but he didn't like the way she dealt with letdowns. It really wasn't his business, but he had to live with the woman or stay holed up in his small apartment, and he wished he could smooth things over for her.

He'd probably shoved too much Bible at her. He knew she'd been raised a Christian from meeting her parents, but she'd lost something along the way. In his opinion, she'd be a happier lady if she settled her disagreement with the Lord. God kept His promises, and Christine could use some reassurance right now.

But he suspected she had deeper issues. Christine's glowing comments about her job left him with questions. She seemed a woman who'd worked hard to get where she was, but she had internal fears. Either she'd failed too often and questioned her own ability, or the job she praised wasn't as fulfilling as she tried to lead him to believe.

What difference did it make? He tossed the napkin onto the table and signaled Jude for more coffee.

The man gave him a nod, then went on to finish whatever he was doing behind the counter.

The lounge was quiet this time of day. The business would probably pick up in the evening, or maybe the first big snowfall had people scrambling to get their sleds ready for use. Only three or four customers had come in to eat, which was unusual for one of the only restaurants open year-round.

Will rarely came to the lounge on Sunday. Usually he ate at Grandma Ella's. He enjoyed those quiet evenings when he'd make a fire in her fireplace and loll around, listening to her stories or watching TV, or sometimes even playing a game of dominos with her. Often she beat the socks off of him. She'd had the mind of a steel trap before the stroke.

Will's thoughts shifted back to his coffee request. When he looked up, he saw Jude wandering over with the pot, so he eased back, not needing to give another call.

"Sorry for the wait," Jude said, and filled Will's cup. He stood a moment, looking at him with questioning eyes. "You don't look too happy."

Will shrugged. "I'm okay."

"How's Ella doing? Troubles? Why no dinner today at the Summers' house?"

"Grandma Ella's okay. Her granddaughter's there to help out. She's been a handful."

"Who? Ella?"

Will grinned at his error. "No. Her granddaughter."

"Teenager?"

His question surprised Will. "No, she's a woman."

Jude set down the pot and made an hourglass shape with his hands. "That kind of woman?"

"I haven't noticed."

Jude let out a guffaw. "Come on. You noticed." He slid into the booth across from Will and folded his arms over his chest. "Either she's old enough to be your mother or ugly as sin. Which is it?"

"Neither." Will focused on his refreshed coffee then lifted the mug to take a drink. The hot liquid burned his tongue, and he pulled the mug back, sloshing coffee onto the table. He grabbed his wrinkled napkin and swiped at the wet spot.

"She's got you addled," Jude said, letting go another loud cackle. "So what's up? She won't give you a second look?"

"That's not it at all. Where's your mind? She's as mean as a cornered opossum." Will heard himself and chuckled at his description. "She's not real happy here taking care of Ella, so she has an attitude." Will told Jude the story about her mother's fall. "So now she's stuck here. She's one of those high-powered business women, I guess."

"I always thought of you as a pretty good businessman yourself."

"Thanks, but it's different. She's in advertising. It's kind of dog-eat-dog, she says. She's apparently afraid to be away too long." His earlier conjecture came to mind.

"Big-city woman in a small town."

Will gave his head a toss. "Something like that." But with his quick response, he pictured Christine's ruddy cheeks and sparkling eyes when she'd climbed off the sled. He saw her surprise and admiration when she'd stepped into his shop, but she'd changed in a moment, sliding right back to her edgy ways when she got the bad news.

"Bring her in. I'll put a smile on her face."

"Right," Will said, making sure Jude heard the sarcasm in his voice.

"Do I see a little jealousy?" Jude asked, slipping from the seat and grabbing the coffeepot from the table.

"Me? You're kidding." Will gave him an evil eye and did a playful toss of his head. "Get out of here."

Jude walked away laughing, while Will sat there trying to make sense out of their conversation. Jealous? Jealous of what? Sure she was a pretty woman, and yes, she could be fun to be with, but he barely knew her and half of what he knew he didn't understand.

He pushed his hip away from the bench and pulled his wallet from his back pocket. If Miss Powers hadn't been so nasty, Will would have been at Grandma Ella's eating a home-cooked meal. *Powers.* Fitting, he thought. He chuckled at his observation, then rose and headed for the cash register to pay his bill.

The next time he saw Christine, he would tell her that was the last time he'd walk away from dinner. He grinned at an idea that came to mind. Maybe he'd give the mighty Miss P a taste of her own medicine.

Will sat in his room, moping. He'd thought of charging into the house and telling Christine what he thought of her behavior, but then he stopped himself. It would do no good. She would be there for a while, and he didn't like stress. He'd had that on the mainland with his dad and life in general. The island had mellowed him. Now he put his energy into creating works of art rather than works of get-even.

He stared at his apartment TV, the program not registering in his mind. He'd turned it on for noise.

He'd hoped he would become distracted, but that hadn't happened.

The room had darkened, and light from the television flickered on the walls. As he rose to turn on a light, he heard a rap at his door.

He snapped on the lamp and grabbed the doorknob. When he pulled it open, he drew back. Christine stood at the door with a dish in her hand. He looked at the plate, then at her. "Yes?"

She stood a moment searching his eyes. "I brought dessert. It's cherry pie. Michigan cherries." She extended the dish. "I made it myself."

He didn't take the plate although he wanted to. His half-eaten burger hadn't filled a corner of his stomach.

"Can I come in?" she asked.

The request surprised him, and he stepped back without thinking.

She took a cautious step forward, still holding out the plate for him.

Will took it and closed the door after her.

Christine stood a moment, scanning the room. "Now that I'm here, I realize I've been in here before, but it's smaller than I remember."

"Thanks for the pie," he said, setting it on the short counter that served as the bulk of his kitchen. He had a compact sink, a microwave over a two-burner stove, and an apartment-size refrigerator in the small kitchenette.

She stood just inside the door, looking as if she wanted to talk but didn't.

"Would you like to sit?" He gestured at a chair.

She took a hesitant step toward it while he moved to his recliner. "Would you like some coffee?"

"Only if you're having some."

"It'll be good with the pie," he said, taking the five steps to the kitchen counter. She didn't speak while he filled the brewer and snapped the switch. By the time he'd slid the canister back in the cabinet and wiped off the spilled grounds, the aroma of coffee filled the air.

He returned to the living room area and slipped into his chair.

She looked at him, her discomfort evident. "I want to apologize—again," she added.

"You're getting good at that," he said, then wished he'd kept his mouth closed when she flinched with his comment.

"I know. I don't mean to behave like this. I—"

"It's your grandmother that I care about, Christine. You can dislike me for whatever reason, but I'm not happy when I see you hurting your grandmother."

Concern spread over her face. "I'm not trying to hurt her. I only—"

"You're not trying to, but I can read your expression, and I'm sure your grandmother can. She knows you don't want to be here, and it makes her feel that she's to blame."

"But she's not to blame. My mother—" She rose in mid-sentence and wandered around the room. "It's no one's fault but my own. I can't control everything that happens in my own life let alone anything that happens in the world."

"None of us can. I used to fight life, but being on the island has helped me to see things in perspective. It's also helped me grow in my faith." He faltered, wanting to be honest. "I sense you don't like me talking about the Bible and God."

She spun around. "That's not true." Her shoulders sagged. "It's not exactly true. I feel guilty when you talk about the Bible. I've drifted so far away from church attendance. My faith has weakened. It all seems so useless to me."

Will rose. "It's not useless. It's the only thing that we can be sure of." He pointed at the chair again. "Please, sit, and I'll get the coffee."

She waited a moment before she ambled back and sank into the cushion. Her lovely face looked stressed, and he wished he could say something. Her concern seemed deep.

When she was seated, he crossed to the cabinet and took out two mugs. "Is there a boyfriend at home that you're worried about?" He glanced at her over his shoulder.

"A boyfriend? No. Not at all. It's my job. There are twenty people waiting for my position at the agency. If I can't be there, I don't know if I'll have a job when I'm able to go back. I can't ask them to give me a month-or-two leave."

He poured the coffee and turned. "Milk? Sugar?"

"Black," she said, rubbing the back of her neck.

He felt sorry for her. No one wanted that kind of job stress. "So what will you do?" He crossed the room and set her coffee on the table beside her.

"I don't know. I have to call tomorrow and see how much they're willing to bend."

While she talked, he pulled the covering off the pie and grabbed a fork, then collected his mug and wandered back to the sofa. "If the firm likes your work—"

She shook her head. "No. It's competitive. We each struggle to present the best promotional package. It's a catfight sometimes." She hesitated. "I can't trust my boss—people steal ideas."

"That's why I like stained glass. It's my idea and no one is there to take credit but me." He drew up his shoulders and gave a faint laugh. "But I also have to carry the brunt of a failure."

Christine seemed to be listening. "Is that why you left the business major?"

"The business world wasn't for me. I knew it in my gut." He pressed his hand against his stomach. "You know how you feel something right here. Right in the core of your being."

She nodded. "Eat your pie. I hope you like it."

He lifted the fork and delved into the dessert, then slipped it into his mouth. The pie was a perfect blend of tart and sweet, just the way he liked it. "It's great." He gestured with his fork.

Christine smiled. "Thanks."

"Let me just add, you make a mean crust."

She said thank-you and grinned, and Will's heart felt good to see her so real again.

"By the way, I accept your apology and I really love your peace offering."

"You're welcome," she said, trying to hide her smile.

Will's mind slid back to the day he'd given Daisy the sugar cube. He hadn't come up with the sweet treat to get Christine eating out of his hand, but she certainly had. He dug into the rich crust and ate another bite of pie.

Chapter Five

Christine sat in her bedroom, staring at her cell phone. She had to call the office, but she didn't want to. Even though she still had a week's vacation, she couldn't rest until she had dealt with the problem.

Her mind kept drifting back to Will's comment the day before. "You know how you feel something right here. Right in the core of your being," he'd said about his work, but Christine wasn't sure if she'd ever felt that certain about anything. She often felt fear in the core of her being.

She fiddled with the cell buttons while trying to phrase her opening sentences. What should she say that would get the point across about her delay without alarming Chet.

Chet. Her stomach twisted. Chet, the man she had trusted and the one who'd stabbed her in the back. The memory of her naiveté suddenly overwhelmed her. As she rehearsed her dialogue, it fell apart, as it did so often when confronting her boss.

Instead of worrying about Chet, she turned her idea to a new direction. If she could work via cell and e-mail for a few days—just as a test—then he would have fewer complaints with her delay in returning to work. The idea sank as fast as it rose, but she had no other plan.

She hit the memory dial and heard the connection. "Sandy? Hi, this is Christine."

"Hey, girlfriend, how's the vacation?"

"It's okay, but—"

"But no handsome men around?"

"That's not the problem."

She chuckled. "Too many choices?"

"No. There's one man—my grandmother's boarder, but he's another issue. Listen to me." She swallowed. "I've run into a problem."

"Problem? What kind?"

Christine summarized her newest challenge in between Sandy's questions and her vocalized groans of sympathy.

"When's the next team meeting?" Christine asked.

"In an hour."

She cringed and looked at her watch. "That soon."

"I thought you were on vacation."

"Yes, I know I'm on vacation, but—"

"Forget the but. Tell me about this boarder. Looks. Age. Prospects."

"I don't know. He's good-looking." Good-looking, beguiling, sweet. "Will owns a store on the island. He's a stained-glass artist."

"Hmm? The artistic type. Clever. Married or—"

"Single. Now can we—"

"Age?"

"I have no idea." She pictured Will's youthful spirit, but he'd accomplished so much she could only speculate. "My age, I suppose. Late thirties maybe, but that has nothing to do with anything. I need to see how I can function long distance, or else how can I impress Chet that I can stay away and still work?"

"That's a hard call, Christine. I don't think it's possible."

Christine tossed the comment aside. "I want to give it a try." She drew up her shoulders. "How about trying a conference call? Do you think that would work?"

Sandy's voice flagged again before she came back with a semipositive comment.

Christine tried to keep up her hopes. "Would you ask the team, then give me a call? I'll sit in on the meeting and see what happens. I have to make this work, Sandy."

"I'll do what I can, Christine, but you're really asking the impossible. What about the visuals—graphics, charts, PowerPoint—"

Her coworker's commiseration did little to assure Christine. "I know, but you can do it."

"Thanks for the vote of confidence," Sandy said.

"Thanks for pitching them the idea for me. I can work on the brochure from here. Tell them that, okay?"

When she'd hung up, she felt defeated. Sandy's reminder of the visuals gnawed at her. The team would spend too much time trying to explain those to her unless… Her spirit lifted. If Sandy could scan the material and send it, she could at least see it on her computer.

Will stopped at the kitchen doorway. "What's wrong?"

Christine shook her head, her face more full of frustration than he'd seen since she arrived. "Nothing."

"For nothing, you look as if you lost your best friend." His heart skipped. "Don't tell me something's wrong with Grandma Ella."

Christine rose and pushed the computer lid closed. "She's fine. The therapist came today, and it tired her. She's napping."

He eyed the computer a moment, then her face, seeing something had upset her. "Did you help Judy with the therapy today?"

"No, I was busy." She heaved a deep sigh. "It was bad timing."

Bad timing. He wondered why Christine didn't understand the importance of therapy. Frisking for a solution, Will wandered to the cookie jar and looked into the empty cavern, then slid the lid back on and moved to the refrigerator. "I can show you what I know. Christine, do you realize the longer it takes her to get back into gear, the harder it'll be?"

As if she hadn't heard, Christine lifted the laptop from the table without a response.

He grabbed an apple from the fridge fruit drawer and closed the door, then leaned his back against it. "You came here to help your grandmother, didn't you?"

"Who are you? The therapy police?" She plopped the computer back onto the table.

"Therapy police?" He laughed.

She looked at him finally and laughed with him. Will loved her smile—when she had one.

"Look, I don't mean to be sharp, but I'm having some problems. I don't know how this is going to work with me on the island and my work in Southfield." Frustration flooded her face. "You don't understand, because your work is here."

"I'm sorry about—" He shook his head, not knowing what to say. Instead he tried a different tack. "Anything I can do to help?"

She stared into space a moment, then gave a single head shake. "Not unless you have a trick form of transportation that can get me to Southfield and back in a couple of minutes."

He slipped into a chair and took a bite of the apple. The skin broke and the loud crack punctuated the silence. "Sorry. I can't help you with that, either."

"No one can," she said, her head lowering.

He waited, then saw her darkened face tinge a brighter shade.

"Or maybe there is." She lifted her eyes to his.

He could see the wheels turning. "What is it?"

"What did you call that service? The place where the therapist works?"

"Vital Care." Disbelieving, he waited for her idea.

"I'll call my dad. I'm sure they have full-time nursing staff. I know it's costly, but Grandma must have insurance and—"

"She only has Medicare. Your folks already checked."

Her head shot upward. "What does that mean?"

"They checked."

"And?"

"I don't want you to bite my head off."

"I won't."

"I don't know all the details, but your dad looked into a temporary full-time caregiver to take over until they returned. It wasn't possible."

She pursed her lips and opened her mouth, then closed it. "I'll still talk to my dad."

"Go ahead." He patted the chair beside him. "Sit for a minute. I have three college years in business. What's your problem at the firm? Maybe I can help."

She looked distrusting at first, then seemed to have second thoughts and sank back into the chair. "It's just difficult. We met today on a conference call." She pulled her cell phone from her pocket and glanced at the phone. "The power's low on my cell." She slipped it back. "It's difficult. Everyone talks at once. I can't see the visuals. I asked Sandy about scanning them or sending attachments ahead of time so I can view them on the computer, but she doesn't have time or access to the ad ideas before the meeting."

Will rallied his courage. "You're on vacation, right?"

"Yes, but that's for little more than a week. I only have a couple more weeks' vacation after that, and I don't want to use them all for—"

"Here's a thought." He managed a smile. "The quicker your grandmother can function alone, the faster you'll get home. Her therapy is vital. Instead of worrying about your job right now, concentrate on helping your grandmother."

Christine's expression caused him to backpedal. "I know your work is your career and your life, but for the next week, let's see how much progress she can make. Between Linda and me, maybe we can take over so you can go home."

Christine's gloom began to fade. "Do you think she'll improve that fast?"

He had to be honest. "A week will give you time to make decisions, and every improvement adds to the possibility."

"You're right," she said.

I am? he almost said aloud. "So with that settled, let's think about dinner." He sent her an approving smile.

He received an arched eyebrow in return.

Christine sat nearby, listening to the therapist's instructions.

"Okay, Ella," Judy said, "now place your arms at

your sides, then slowly lift them over your head and then lower them. We'll do this ten times today."

Watching her grandmother's struggle gnawed at Christine's emotions. Something so simple appeared very difficult. Ella raised her right arm, but it seemed forever before the left rose above the mattress.

"Good," Judy said. "Now again."

Christine averted her gaze and looked out the window at the dancing snow. Snow. Time had flown. Thanksgiving had passed the week before, and now Christmas seemed on their doorstep. She had so much to do for the holiday. She hadn't finished her shopping, and nothing seemed open on the island.

"Do you understand, Christine?"

Judy's voice jerked her back to the therapy. "Yes, ten times over her head."

Her frown gave Christine a warning she'd let her attention drift too far.

"Then she will sit up and do ten more." She supported Ella's back and helped her raise her left arm. "After a couple, she can try it herself. Right, Ella?"

"Right," Ella said, with a look of despair.

Christine nodded. "Ten times lying down and ten sitting up."

"Yes, and then on Friday, add five more. And I want you to pick up a jigsaw puzzle. That'll be great exercise for Ella's hands and fingers. It aids dexterity."

"A jigsaw puzzle."

"Yes. They probably have them at the drugstore."

Christine's thoughts left the jigsaw puzzle and shifted to Will. He'd tried so hard to help her, and she had been terribly ungrateful. He made her laugh and forget her troubles, but she fought him every step. Why? She shook her head, having no answer except the one she didn't want to face—envy of his relationship with her grandmother.

Christine's focus drifted back to her grandmother's quivering limbs. Sadness washed over her.

Judy helped Ella rise. "And now we're going to do laps."

"Laps?" That statement triggered Christine's attention. "Where?"

"From the living room through the foyer into the kitchen and around the table and back." She turned to Ella. "You'll use your walker, but soon I want you on a cane. You want to get well, don't you?"

"Do I look stupid?" Ella said.

Christine laughed.

"Now, now, Ella. You're a smart lady," Judy said, "and that's why I know you can do this. But you must have someone work with you. Don't try walking with the cane alone for a while."

The truth of the situation sank into Christine's head. She couldn't walk away and leave her grandmother unless she had professional help, and if Will had been accurate, that seemed hopeless. Maybe he'd been wrong.

As the thought drifted into her mind, Christine

heard the hallway door open and close, and Will appeared in her grandmother's bedroom doorway. "How's it going?"

The scent of winter rode in on his jacket—a crispy fragrance of outdoors and fresh air.

"I'm going to be doing a few pirouettes before you know it," Ella said. "Just you wait and see."

"I never doubted that," Will said. He strode toward Judy. "Are you finished?"

"We'll do some laps, but I think Christine's done."

"That's who I wanted," he said. "Are you going to be here for a few more minutes?"

Judy nodded. "Another half hour or so."

"Great," he said, running his fingers through his snow-dampened hair. "I want to show Christine a couple of things if I can steal her."

"She's all yours." Judy looked from Christine to Will and back again. "Are you taking her to the tree-lighting ceremony tonight? It's a beautiful sight."

"Tree lighting? I hadn't—"

"At dusk," Ella said, gesturing with her good arm. "Christine would enjoy that, Will. I'm sure Linda will come in to stay for an hour while you go."

Christine's focus wasn't on the tree lighting. Instead she wondered why Will wanted to steal her, but anything seemed better than watching her grandmother grimace with pain.

"No problem for me," Judy said, supporting Ella's calf as she lifted her leg. "Take a good half hour."

Will beckoned to Christine.

She rose without argument and followed him into the hallway, admiring his broad shoulders yet concerned about his coy smile. "Where are you taking me?"

"Put on your coat and boots. It's lesson time."

Lesson time? "I've had about as many lessons as I need for one day. I'm a full-fledged therapist as we speak."

Will grinned, and the look won her over.

"I have something in mind besides therapy." He pointed toward the foyer. "Coat and boots."

"Is that an order?"

He nodded and led the way.

"Daisy's on the mainland, right? I'm not learning to horseback ride."

"No, but you should learn how to use the sled in case you need to get away when I'm not here. I'll just show you how to start it and take it for a short spin." He gestured toward the doorway. "There's new snow, and it'll be a smooth ride."

"Please, Will, I don't want—"

"Shush!" He walked up behind her and slipped his hand over her mouth, his face against her hair. She heard him draw a deep breath. "You smell like cookies. Vanilla wafers?"

"It's my lotion," she said, feeling his warm breath on her cheek. "And I suppose I'd better bake some cookies, since I've seen you looking into the empty container."

He turned her around, his eyes capturing hers. "I like cookies."

But his eyes said he liked her, and the feeling wavered down her limbs. She looked away and wrapped a scarf around her neck. "Let's get this over with. If I break a hip, then you're going to be nursemaid to everyone."

"You won't break anything but a few hearts, Christine."

A few hearts. Her pulse skipped, and she gave a sarcastic laugh, hoping their conversation would get back to normal. She hadn't met a man in a long time who could rattle her equilibrium like Will.

He guided her through the kitchen to the porch. Her grandmother's smaller sled sat beside his. She eyed it as if it were a rocket and she were going to the moon.

Though the snow had deepened, the sun felt warmer than the last time Christine had faced a snowmobile. She squinted at the light glinting from the fresh powdery crystals, then looked into the clear blue sky. She understood why David had written the Psalms. On days like this, if she were a poet, she would write a beautiful praise.

Her thoughts of the Lord surprised Christine as she moved through the snow. Perhaps a place like the island gave her more time to think about things other than competition and survival in the mad rush of life at home.

"I'll warn you," Christine said, "I can never start a lawn mower."

Will grinned. "This one is different." He stood beside the smaller sled, dangling a key. "It has a regular ignition. No pull starter."

"Whew!" She adored his cute grin. "I'm relieved."

Will patted the seat. She slipped into it and felt like a seasoned sledder.

He poked the key into the ignition. "Now pull out the choke about halfway." He pointed to the right side of the handlebars. "It's that tab marked by the circle with a diagonal line through it."

Will was leaning so close to her, she breathed in his subtle scent of spice. He turned to look at her, his breath puffing in a white stream and blending with hers.

She steadied her emotions and did as he told her.

"That's right," he said.

His face, spotlighted by the sun, looked so handsome in the bright light. The creases she'd seen around his eyes seemed to have vanished.

"Now," he said, turning back to the gauges, "when you turn the key and the engine sounds steady, push in the choke." He chuckled. "Hopefully the sled will stay running on its own."

"Okay," Christine said, looking at all the gadgetry in front of her and doing as he'd told her. The sound of the engine hammered the afternoon air. She glanced at the floorboard. "But where's the gas pedal and brake?"

He brushed his palm against her hair. "You're too funny. It's here." He pointed to the handlebars. "Put your hands here and find the lever on the right side. That's the throttle. Use your thumb to gain speed."

"And the brake?" she asked, feeling more panicky.

"The lever on the left. The sled will slow automatically by releasing pressure on the throttle, especially in soft snow. That's why I thought you should have the lesson today."

"Throttle on the right. Brake on the left."

"That's it. And remember to lean into the turn. If you don't, you can flip over."

"Thanks," she said, raising her hands in the air. "That's enough lesson for me."

He caught her hand and gave it a squeeze. "Come on. Be a sport." He cupped his other hand around hers, and the warmth penetrated her gloves.

"If you want independence, you'll need to ride this thing."

Will walked away, slipped on his helmet and started the engine. He sat a moment before rolling forward and stopping beside her. "Ready?"

She covered her head with the helmet and drew in a hasty breath, her voice catching in her throat. She could only nod.

"Let's go." He motioned forward and glided down the driveway to the snow-covered road.

Christine followed his instructions as best she could remember, then jerked forward and stalled.

Will grinned and waited.

She started the engine again, and this time kept it going. As she rolled forward, Will shot onto the street.

Christine eased out to the road, fear and adventure knotted in every sinew. She pressed the throttle, and the sled gunned forward. Soon she was behind Will, feeling like a baby bird learning to fly.

The wind nipped at her nose, and each breath seemed to crystalize inside her lungs, but it awakened her spirit. She heard her laughter sail on the air. She couldn't remember feeling so free and happy in a long time.

Ahead Will slowed, then made a great loop into a snow-covered field and headed back up Cupid's Pathway. The street name made her grin. It sounded like a children's tale of princes and princesses.

In only a few minutes, they returned home, and she felt disappointed the lesson was over. She parked and climbed off, her heart thundering in her chest and pride billowing in her heart. "Not bad," she said, pulling off the helmet and shaking her hair free.

Will hurried to her side, drew her into his arms, lifted her above the ground, then plopped her back to earth.

She caught her breath, stunned at their play.

"You were wonderful," he said. "The best student I've ever had."

"And how many is that?"

"One, but you were very good."

"Thanks. It was fun."

His gaze searched hers and made her nervous. He was an attractive man.

"You look like a teenager," Will said. "Look at

those rosy cheeks and that sparkle in your eyes. You're a beautiful woman, Christine."

He'd taken her aback with his comment. "Forget that teenage comment. I'm far from that. I'll accept the rosy cheeks. I can feel them burning."

Will tilted her face upward and studied her again. "You're timeless, I'd say."

She felt her heart flutter, and the sensation set her on edge. What was she thinking? She checked her watch. "I think it's time to get back in."

He rested his hand on her shoulder. "Good job on the sled."

"Thanks."

"I'll put it in the stable and be heading back to work. I'll pick you up later for the tree lighting." He gave her a wink and pivoted away toward the sleds.

"See you later." She gave a quick wave while her heart did a loop-the-loop.

The Christmas tree stood near the chamber of commerce building on Main Street. Christine's eagerness grew as she watched the schoolchildren's excitement as they gathered around the tree. Will stood behind her, his hands on her shoulders.

The evening wind felt nippier than what she'd experienced earlier in the day; a chill prickled along her spine. Will moved beside her and slid his arm around her. He gave her an easy smile, and she smiled back, for once comfortable with his closeness.

Snowflakes began to fall like a picture-perfect

Christmas scene. They drifted on the breeze and twirled on the chilling air. Will held her close, and she warmed at his touch.

The ceremony began, and soon the tree lights glowed, with cheers and oohs from those who were gathered. The friendly chatter and handshakes felt so different from the life she led at home. She shifted to leave, but Will held her close. "Now we sing carols."

"Really?"

She saw the glow in his eyes and guessed the same glow was in hers. The music began and the children's voices filled the crisp air with songs like "Joy to the World," "Away in a Manger," and "Silent Night."

With each song, Will's baritone voice joined the singers. At first, she sang with timidity, then found her voice lifting along with his. Joyous sounds filled with the spirit of the season—a kind of music and feeling she'd only thought of in dreams.

"Fun?" he asked.

"Wonderful." She gazed into his eyes, sparkling brighter than the tree lights, and in the joy of the moment she had an urge to kiss him. "Thank you," she said, tiptoing up to plant a quick kiss on his lips.

Though he looked surprised, he smiled. "Tell me what else I can do to win another one of those."

She chuckled liked a schoolgirl, then caught herself. What was she doing? She was Christine Powers, businesswoman, devoted to her job, a dynamo in advertising. How could a tree-lighting ceremony three hundred miles from home turn her into a giggly teenager?

Will bent and kissed her cheek. "I'm glad you're having a good time. I won't forget tonight."

She looked at the snowflakes resting on his hair, his beguiling smile, and the warmth in his eyes. She would never forget tonight, either.

Chapter Six

"So Mom's doing well, you think?"

Christine's shoulders relaxed hearing her father's positive response.

"Can I talk with her?"

"Just a minute. I'll wake her."

"No, Dad. I can talk another time."

"How's your grandmother?"

"She's doing fine. I'm learning how to help her with the therapy. I think she's improving every day…so I have a question."

She heard silence on the line.

"This is theoretical, but let's say I can't get a leave or I can't work from here, and my boss insists I return. If that happened, I was thinking that—"

"Christine, did you ask for an extension?"

"No, but I'm afraid that—"

"Wait. Don't you have more leave time?"

"Yes, I have a couple more weeks' vacation, but I'd like to have some time during the summer to—"

"You know there's no one else to send." His voice was weighted with frustration. "Chad's—"

"I know Chad can't leave his family and come here at the holidays. I understand, but—" Her father's comment about her married brother bristled down her back. "I feel I'm being punished for being single. I have a life, too, and…"

This time her father didn't stop her, and she didn't know where to go.

"What about professional full-time care for Grandma? She must have insurance, and I thought—"

She listened to the same thing Will had told her.

"That doesn't seem right," she said.

"Do you want us to put your grandmother in a home?"

"No." Her hand had tensed on her cell phone, and she longed to lay it down, to disconnect, to cancel the call if she could. The conversation had gone as badly as she imagined it would. She asked herself why she'd bothered.

"I'll call my boss next Monday, and see what I can do."

The conversation bogged down with her mother's prognosis—two months or more before she would be able to travel. When Christine hung up from her father, tears filled her eyes. She couldn't stay that long, and she saw no other solution.

Rarely had Christine prayed in recent years. Today

she bowed her head and talked with God. The Lord had ways of solving problems that a human couldn't even imagine. She had to depend on God's mercy.

Feeling calmer, Christine headed downstairs, putting on her I'm-just-fine expression. At the bottom of the steps, she heard her grandmother's voice talking to her.

"I didn't hear you, Grandma Summers. I was upstairs." She stepped into the living room and stopped. Her grandmother was speaking on the telephone, her face lit with a smile.

"Who was that?" Christine asked when she'd hung up.

"One of the circle ladies from church. Some of them thought I looked good when they saw me on Sunday."

"You did. I told you."

"Tomorrow they're coming to visit and bringing some casseroles for our dinners. I don't know how many, but I thought you'd like to hear that."

Christine didn't know which she enjoyed hearing more, the news about the prepared dinners or the ladies' visit.

"And you'll have some free time to enjoy yourself for a change," her grandmother added.

That thought had already crossed her mind. "That's thoughtful, Grandma, but the best thing is to see the smile on your face."

"I hadn't realized how much I miss my church friends," Ella said. "A few came to see me in the hospital, and I had many cards and some food gifts when your folks were here, but you know how it is. Time passes, and it's easy to forget about those who are sick. I must keep that in mind when I'm doing well again."

"I have no doubt you will," Christine said, remembering the vow her grandmother had made when she was a girl. "Are you ready to tackle your therapy?"

The grin faded.

"The stronger you become the faster you'll be up and active again." Will's words spilled from her as his face rose in her thoughts. He always said the right thing.

"I know," Ella said, giving a toss of her head. "Let's get at it."

Will glanced at his desk calendar to check the deadline date for a stained-glass window he was making for a customer. He'd selected clear glass of varying textures to complement the bevel cluster. The windows were big sellers.

As his eyes shifted over the November dates, he realized his error and flipped the page to December. Time was flying, and he'd promised to have a table at the Christmas Bazaar the coming weekend. He drew back, amazed at how forgetful he'd become. He'd mentioned the event to Christine only days earlier.

His mind wandered, knowing he needed to select his art pieces and box them to transport to the Community Hall. Too much to do, and too little time. He scanned the December dates again, noting he had plenty of time to complete the customer's beveled window, but what else waited to be done?

As the calendar came into view again, his thoughts took a detour. He scanned the excellent still life photograph of the stone church on Grand Hill, the evergreen branches weighted with snow against the gray stone and the one bright spot—a cardinal sitting on the fir. He'd wanted to spend a day taking photos for the annual calendar contest that the island held each year. The judging would be at the Winter Festival in February, and if he wanted to enter, he needed to get the photographs taken. He rubbed his neck, wondering which way to turn. Christine had thrown his schedule out of whack.

He eyed his watch. Lunchtime. His chest tightened with awareness. Normally he'd stay at the studio and eat a cold sandwich or heat up a commercial microwave soup, but lately, he'd taken time to go back home to eat. He didn't have to question his motives. Christine. She filled his mind.

Grabbing his jacket, he switched the light off with his other hand and headed outside. He locked the door, jumped on his sled and headed up Market Street. Home seemed to pull him like a magnet.

The day seemed perfect—a crisp breeze but an abundance of sunshine. The scenery flashed past, and as he neared his apartment, his pulse raced. He knew he was being foolish. He already suspected Christine was older and wiser than he. He certainly wasn't the kind of man who would interest her, so why open himself for rejection?

The question led him into a new line of thought. He enjoyed her company. He hadn't met any younger woman on the island that captured his interest as Christine had. Maybe it was her spunk or her business prowess. He respected that. More likely he was drawn to the Christine she let him see when she let down her guard. She could make him laugh, and he loved that. Why not enjoy her company while she was here and let it go at that?

He let the answer slip away, aware of the flashing warning sign he didn't want to face. He drove up Grandma Ella's driveway and entered through the back door. A tangy scent greeted him along with a smile from Christine.

"What's cookin'?" He slipped off his shoes in the back hallway and hung his jacket on a chair near the door.

"Sloppy Joes. I haven't eaten one for years."

He stood close to her, enjoying the rich aroma of the meat-and-tomato blend, along with her nearness. "Can I help?"

"You can open the buns."

He spotted the package on the counter and opened the cellophane. Before he removed them from the wrapper, he moved to the sink to wash his hands.

"And you can get the chips. They're on the fridge."

Will set out three plates, placed an open bun on each, then tore open the bag of potato chips. "I'm glad I came home."

"So am I," she said. "Grandma Summers has

friends coming in tomorrow, so I'll have a couple of free hours. I need to do some Christmas shopping. Any ideas?"

His mind surged to the calendar he'd perused earlier. "The Christmas Bazaar is Saturday at the Community Center. You can pick up some handmade items and even have an ice-cream sundae while you're there."

"A bazaar? I'm not sure that's the best place to buy quality gifts." She reached for a plate.

He moved closer and held the dish while she piled the meat mixture onto the bun. "Sure it is. Wait until you see the great things they have. I have a booth there."

"Your stained glass?" She stood transfixed with the spoonful of meat hovering over the plate.

"Smaller items. I will probably bring a few windows, sun catchers, Christmas ornaments, some jewelry."

"Jewelry?"

"It's made with fused glass. You'll be surprised." He turned and placed the dish on the table. "Lots of things. We have a talented island. Scarves, mittens, winter caps." He fought the temptation to run his fingers through her waves. "You could use a cap."

"If I go, I'll have to find someone to stay with—"

"Bring her along. She needs to get out. You're doing her laps, right?"

She drew back. "Yes, Mr. Therapy Police. I had her doing laps today."

He grinned. "The more she realizes what she's missing the harder she'll work to get better."

Christine nodded. "She mentioned today how much she misses everyone."

"Going will make her happy then. I think the walker will work for Saturday. There are benches where she can sit and visit."

"Good idea." Christine turned off the burner and slid the pot off the heat. "Can you bring in Grandma while I get the drinks?"

"Sure thing," he said, whistling a rambling tune as he headed into the living room.

Ella grinned at him when he came through the doorway She looked sunnier than he'd seen her in days, and it made him feel good. "Lunchtime." He strode across the room and plopped her walker in front of her. "If you don't get walking, you'll miss the best Sloppy Joes ever made."

"I smell them," she said, struggling to rise with only one strong hand.

He let her struggle, knowing that the more she forced herself to do, the better off she'd be. When she'd managed to grab hold of the walker with both hands, she shuffled forward while he stayed close by her side. He could see the difference even in the past couple days that Christine had been making her do laps two or three times a day.

When they gathered around the table, Ella reached toward Christine to take her hand. Will noticed and grasped Ella's left, but Ella didn't begin the prayer. Her eyes were focused on the broken circle. Will eyed Christine, and she reached over and took his hand.

Grandma Ella began the prayers, thanking God for the day, the food, family and friends. Will tried to concentrate, but his mind skipped off on its own to the pleasant sensation of Christine's delicate hand in his, her tapered fingers nestled against his palm.

"And Lord, we ask You for patience and persever-ance. We don't always understand Your ways, but we know You are directing our steps. Keep us mindful of Your mercy and grace. Keep us attentive to Your love and forgiveness. Amen."

In the silence as each of them delved into the savory sandwich, Will's mind marched back to Christine's sweeter manner. He liked what he'd seen the past two days—the sled ride and today the cama-raderie. Grandma Ella's words about love and for-giveness sank into his thoughts. How long would it take before he and Christine might be real friends?

He looked up and saw Christine watching him. When they were alone, he planned to invite her on his photography venture. He wondered if she might inspire something unique and amazing in his photo-graphs. She'd already inspired his imagination.

"Now don't you worry," Darlene Baxter said. "We'll keep Ella busy for a couple of hours, and then I thought I'd stay on a while and help her with her therapy. She can tell me what to do."

"That's so nice of you," Christine said.

"Ella says you're devoting too much time to her, and she wants you to enjoy yourself."

Christine winced with the comment. "You're too kind, Mrs. Baxter. Thanks again." Guilt pressed against her shoulders, knowing she'd only been devoted to her grandmother the past couple of days. Before she had only whined.

"I'm going to run a few errands while you're here."

"Have fun," Ella said, as Christine strolled into the foyer. She paused to look out the door's beveled window and saw Will pulling into the driveway.

Perfect timing, she thought, as she slipped on her jacket and boots.

Before she'd finished, he gave a tap and opened the door. "Looks like I'm right on time."

"I have to find my scarf and gloves." She tiptoed to peek onto the top shelf.

Will came forward and reached over her head. "Here you go," he said, pulling them down from the top shelf.

She wrapped the plaid blue scarf around her neck— one that belonged to her grandmother—and Will took the end and gave an extra pull. Christine loosened the scarf, giving his gleeful expression a frown.

He opened the door, and she slipped on her gloves as she stepped outside. "Bye, Grandma," she called.

Muffled voices sent back a greeting as Will closed the door. "It's a great day," he said. "This past week's been wonderful. Would you like to have a diversion before you run your errands?"

He'd piqued her interest. "What kind of diversion?"

"A photo shoot."

"Photo shoot?"

"For the island calendar. They hold a contest during the Winter Festival and select twelve photos taken of scenes on the island for next year's calendar."

"Do you have one in this year?"

His smile faded. "Never. So I thought maybe you'd inspire me. Bring me luck, maybe."

"How long?"

He shrugged. "As long as it takes."

"I have only an hour."

She noticed he didn't comment. He ushered her toward his sled, and she settled onto the seat, then scooted back. Once he was on, he maneuvered the sled from the driveway, and they were off.

They headed into town and stopped to take photos of a streetlamp adorned with a Christmas wreath, then off to Market Street where Will photographed the quiet setting looking toward the fort. The still beauty wrapped around Christine's spirit.

Will looked content, setting his aperture for the best lighting and distance. He moved from one angle to another. He shifted beneath a tree and aimed the camera upward through the snow-burdened branches to the amazing blue sky.

"I bet that was beautiful," Christine said, shifting her weight and bumping a limb.

Before Will could move, an avalanche of snow fell from one branch to the next and blanketed him in a snow pile. "Thanks," he said, jumping away and grabbing a cloth to wipe the camera.

"I'm sorry."

He shook his head and chucked her cheek. "Forgiven. No damage as long as I get the snow off fast."

She hovered over him, fearful that she'd destroyed his camera. He raised it without her expecting and snapped her photo.

"Why did you do that? I wasn't smiling."

"You looked lovely—concerned and guilty. That's just the way I like you."

She folded her arms. "No photos unless I have a warning."

"Okay," he said. "Be warned." He moved the f-stop and snapped another photo.

"I thought the calendar was scenery."

"It is, but I took these for me."

"Why?"

"To remember you by."

Her breath left her for a moment, realizing one day she would be gone. Her job and her life waited for her in Southfield, not the island.

He stood a minute, looking into the sky.

"Something wrong?"

"Thinking."

She waited beside him and thought, too, about the fun she'd had since she stopped fighting Will and her grandmother's care, but she knew that in a few more days, she had to face reality. If her boss didn't approve a leave—and she feared he wouldn't just for spite—she would be in a bind. Chet would love to get her out of the company. But she had the goods on him, and he knew it.

"What are you thinking?" she asked finally.

"I want something unique. Special. This time of year my photos will be for snow months—November through March. Everyone does the Christmas wreath, the fort, the snow piled in the fields. I want a different idea. Something other than Thanksgiving, Christmas or New Year's Eve."

"That leaves February," Christine said.

"What happens in February other than a short month that takes forever?" he asked.

"Valentine's Day."

His head shot upward. "Hearts, flowers, cupids, love."

"How about a photo on Cupid's Pathway?" she asked.

His eyebrows raised. "Okay. You have something there, but what. Not just a street view. That's not original. Something to do with Valentine's Day."

"A heart."

"Whose?"

She chuckled. "Not mine. A heart…in the snow."

"Yes!" He twirled around on one heel as if spinning would bring an idea. "Drawn by a finger." He looked at her hands. "With red gloves. Instead of carving a heart with initials on a tree, a girl spells it in snow."

"I like it," she said. "We can find fresh snow near the house."

"But color? Is the glove enough?" He snapped

his finger. "Let me run into the shop a minute." He
beckoned her to follow.

They hurried up the road a couple of shops, and
Will opened the door and ran into the back. Christine waited by the door gazing around the room. She
could purchase some wonderful Christmas gifts from
Will's shop. She headed for a display, but he reappeared, looking empty-handed, and waved her
toward the door.

"I thought you—"

He patted his pocket. "I have what I need. Wait
and see."

She followed him outside, and when he locked the
door, they climbed on the sled and raced up Cadotte
Avenue to Hoban Road into Harrisonville. When
they turned right onto Cupid's Pathway, Will slowed
and scanned the roadside. "I need fresh snow."

She pointed to a patch of open snow, unblemished
and glistening in the winter sun.

"That's great," he said, pulling the sled to the
road's edge and turning it off.

He stepped out and grabbed his camera.

Christine sat on the sled, watching him move from
right to left, close, then farther away using his zoom
lens. He crouched down and focused on the snow,
then rose again and tossed a stick onto one area and
studied it through the lens.

"What are you doing?" Christine called out.

"Checking for light and shadow." He beckoned
to her.

She slipped off the sled and headed his way, tucking her hands into her pockets away from the nippy air.

"Look through the lens at the stick," he said, handing her the camera.

She put her eye against the viewfinder while Will stood close beside her, his hand resting on her shoulder. She located the broken limb. Sunlight from the left caused a definite shadow on the snow. "The stick leaves a fine shadow."

"It will broaden as the sun lowers in the sky, but it's enough." He studied her face as he took the camera from her.

"Interesting," Will said, wondering if he meant the shadows or her.

He hung the camera on his neck, then moved to an unmarred snowbank. He crouched and took his finger and drew a large heart on the snow. The shadow highlighted it with a fine line of gray.

Christine admired the almost perfect heart. She waited to see what was next, curious about what he'd brought from the studio.

Will paused a moment, looking through the lens again, and then squatted and marked his initials— W. L.—into the snow. Below the letters he marked a plus sign. Finally, he rose.

"Your turn." He glanced at her hands. "Where are your gloves?"

"In here," she said, pulling her hands from her pockets.

"Good. Now crouch like I did and draw your

initials, but don't lift your finger when you get to the end of the letter *P*."

Rattled, she turned to him. "You want me to use my initials?"

"Sure." He gave her a wink. "Why not?"

She had no answer for that, but it didn't seem appropriate for her to be making a heart with their initials. The whole idea unsettled her.

"Go ahead," he said, standing back and focusing.

If she refused, she'd be making a big deal out of nothing, so she knelt and stretched her arm over the heart and scratched her initials beneath the plus sign. C. P. She heard the lens click, then click again.

"Hold it," he said, shifting and snapping two more shots. "Okay. That's it."

She rose, her legs feeling tingly from lack of blood and from the cold.

"Want to see?" he asked.

"See? But you brought something with you, I thought."

"Red glass globs. I thought I'd outline the heart, but I don't need them. "Look at it." He beckoned her.

She hurried to his side.

"Here." He handed her the digital camera, hit a button, and the photograph appeared. The effect startled her—the stark white snow, the shadow heart and initials, then her bright red finger. "It's really great, Will. Beautiful in its simplicity."

"And perfect for February. I'll title it *Love on Cupid's Pathway*."

Love on Cupid's Pathway. She looked back at the heart and their initials and felt a flush rise up her neck. "We'd better go, don't you think?"

He grasped her hand and pulled her closer. "Are you upset?"

"No, I—I'm just looking at the time." She glanced at her watch.

"Thanks for the inspiration," he said.

She saw it coming and didn't move. Will bent over and planted a kiss on her cold cheek. The warmth radiated through her, and she had to fight the desire to turn her cheek and kiss his mouth.

Chapter Seven

"I have a matching bracelet if you're interested," Will said to customer Myra Holt. He dug beneath the table, located it and handed it to her.

"This is gorgeous, Will. I love the colors."

"Thanks." His attention drifted toward the doorway, looking for Christine, then back to Myra.

She eyed the price tag and didn't flinch. "Let me get Gus, and see what he says. I'll be right back." She sent him a smile and headed down the aisle looking for her husband.

Will leaned back in the folding chair, grabbing a moment's break before the next customer arrived. Everyone knew everyone on the island, so the Christmas Bazaar seemed one big party.

A woman passed wearing a red jacket, and the color took him back to yesterday afternoon when he'd had the nerve to insist Christine write her initials in the snow. She'd flushed, he'd noticed, and he wasn't sure if she was embarrassed or flattered. He hoped it was the latter.

Something about Christine had worked its way into his thoughts and wound around his heart as tightly as tendrils on a morning glory. He felt the spiral squeeze, and his pulse raced. The dream was ridiculous. He wanted to ask Grandma Ella Christine's age, but he didn't have the nerve. Anyway, it was difficult to talk with Ella alone. Christine always seemed to hover nearby like flies at a picnic.

Will grinned to himself. He loved her hovering, but not when he hoped to talk privately to her grandmother. Will wasn't sure what difference it would make, but sometimes age bothered women. He liked her maturity. At times, she seemed girlish, like the times they'd spent on the sled when her smile lit up the sky and her laughter rekindled his longing for someone to share his life.

Will knew the day would come when she would leave. Maybe sooner than he thought. On Monday, she'd said she had to call her boss. Could he say no to a family's need? She'd hinted that she had a difficult relationship with him, and Will had wondered what that was about. Had it been a romance or some work-related conflict? He drew in a deep breath. So many things he would probably never know.

"Here it is," Myra said, returning. She held the bracelet and pendant toward her husband.

The man looked at it with a blank face, obviously

not interested. "If you like it, buy it," he said, after a cursory look.

"Are you sure? You could wrap it for Christmas," Myra said.

"Wouldn't that be dumb? You know what it is."

"Maybe by then I'd forget."

Gus brushed her off with a hand motion. "Buy it. Enjoy it."

Her glum look brightened, and she turned back to Will. "He said it's okay."

"I'm sure you'll enjoy these pieces, Myra." Will slipped them onto the cotton and put a lid on the white nondescript box he used for the jewelry. He pulled out the gold foil Sea of Glass sticker and added it to the top. When he lifted his head, Christine stood beside Myra. He felt a smile grow on his face.

"Hi," he said. "I wondered if you would come."

"It took a little longer getting Grandma here."

Will realized he was still holding Myra's package. He handed it to her. "Myra, this is Christine. She's Ella Summers's granddaughter from Lower Michigan."

The women greeted each other while Will's gaze wandered over Christine's form. She carried her jacket on her arm, and he could see her attire. She'd worn a sweater the color of autumn leaves—shades of orange, coral, red and gold—that highlighted her honey hair and hazel eyes. She looked like an Indian-summer day.

Myra stood between them for a moment, and

when the conversation didn't go anywhere, she said goodbye and headed in the direction Gus had gone.

"What do you think?" Will asked.

"About the bazaar?"

He nodded.

"It's nice. I've only been here a few minutes."

"Where's your grandmother?"

"She found a seat by one of her circle ladies. She's selling quilted things—toss pillows and baby blankets."

She glanced over her shoulder as if checking on her grandmother, and Will rose and came out from behind the table.

"I have a friend who'll sit in for me for a while when you'd like some ice cream."

She turned back. "Thanks. I'll pass for now. Maybe later. I want to see what you're selling."

He backed away and allowed her room to study the glass pieces he had on display. She admired his work, and he enjoyed hearing her oohs and aahs.

"I'd like to buy a few things for gifts. It's beautiful stuff, Will." She eyed the table again and then shifted to the jewelry. "How do you do this?" She studied the pendant, holding it to the light. "Is it really glass?"

"Fused glass. I have some fluted bowls and dishes back at the studio made in the same way."

"Really?" She shifted to a bracelet, then earrings. "It's amazing. Tell me how it's made."

"I heat it in a kiln to various degrees until it's

fused. You can see some is rough—the glass has melted together and adheres, but you can feel the ridges of each color." He lifted her hand and ran her finger along the piece of glass.

He loved the feel of her hand in his, her fingers warm and soft like smooth glass cooling from the kiln.

"Or you can fire it at a higher temperature, around eighteen hundred degrees, and then—"

"You get this," she said, raising a pendant, the colors melded together in one smooth piece."

"That's it," he said, squeezing the hand that he held in his. His confidence rose, knowing she hadn't pulled away from him. That had been real progress with Christine.

"If you come to my studio sometime, I'll show you how to make glass beads like these."

She grasped the strand of flowing beadwork and turned it in her hand. "I love this. The colors and—" She looked at him in what he could only call admiration.

"You have a gold mine here, Will. I'm amazed." She laid the necklace down on the velvet-covered table. "How does this work? Do you donate some of your profits?"

He shook his head. "It's all donated. I'm giving these items away."

"Giving? You're kidding."

"That's the spirit of Christmas. The money's divided five ways—the four churches on the island and the medical center."

"But this is worth so much." She gestured toward the display.

"The churches and medical center are worth much more. Where would we be without them?"

"I suppose." Her eyebrows lifted as she turned to view a sun catcher, then hung it back on the stand. She paused a moment. "I have some ideas for you."

He managed to hold his stance, but his instinct was to draw back. Ideas meant interference. He wanted no part of strategies. His father admired those. Will grimaced inwardly, realizing, instead of interfering, perhaps she had a jewelry design idea. He changed the subject.

"Visit the studio, and I'll show you how to make glass beads. They're easy, really."

She grinned. "For you maybe."

He drew her closer and gave her a squeeze. "You'll just have to trust me. Now stay right here, and I'll get someone to cover my booth so we can take a walk."

Christine watched him walk away, her mind spilling out marketing ideas. She turned again to study the jewelry, wondering how much promotion he did and what yearly income he netted. She could double it. He could hire other workers to do the simpler steps—like the bead making—and he could use his time for the artistic creativity.

Her skin prickled with excitement, anxious to tell him about her thoughts. When she looked at the crowd and the buzz of activity around her, she wondered if this was a practical time to talk. She could see Will in the distance, cornered by two people who seemed determined to carry on a lengthy conversation. He'd gestured her way, but that hadn't stopped them.

Small towns. She'd never seen anything like the friendliness she'd noticed here. Besides church, in stores and on the street, people called to Will by name, and not just a few, but about everyone he passed.

Even yesterday, the postman had called her by name. The postman. Obviously she had a postman in Royal Oak, but to have him call her Christine seemed beyond her comprehension. She didn't know a tenth of the people who worked in the office building where Creative Productions had their suite let alone a whole town.

Finally, she saw Will make his way down the aisle. After two more stops, this time shorter, he returned to her side, and within seconds, so did a woman.

"Christine, this is Janet Deacon. She works for me part-time in the store during the tourist season."

Christine took the woman's hand in greeting. She was an attractive lady, perhaps her age, and Christine eyed Will to see if she was more than a part-time employee, but Will's eyes were on her, and she let the question fade. When her mind made queries like that one, it set her on edge.

"We'll only be a half hour or so," Will said.

"No problem, Will. I'm happy to help." She sent him a smile, which he returned, then he took Christine's arm and led her away from the table.

"Where's the booth you left Grandma Ella at?" he asked, craning his neck to look along the busy aisles.

"This way," she said, pointing.

He walked beside her, stopped every few minutes for conversation and introductions. Christine figured they'd never get to the ice-cream area.

Finally her grandmother came into view. "How are you doing?" Christine asked as she approached.

"Okay," Ella said, looking a little tired but happy.

"You want to leave?"

"No, I'm fine for a while. Enjoy yourself."

"How about an ice-cream sundae?" Will asked, patting her shoulder in the gentlest way, which made Christine's heart surge. He would be a good father, she could tell.

"We had a sundae a few minutes ago, but thanks."

"You did?" Christine asked.

"Darlene's son brought them to us. The best ice cream. Fattening, but who cares?" Ella said.

Christine grinned. "I care."

Will shook his head. "Does this lovely woman look overweight to you?"

Darlene chuckled. "No, not even without love in my eyes."

The comment startled Christine, but she forced herself to laugh. What were people thinking? She studied Darlene, who prattled on about her son and her sales. What did the woman see in Will's eyes? What did she see in Christine's?

"Ready?" Will asked, clasping her arm.

"Sure," she said, the word nearly inaudible. She needed to get a grip. Darlene didn't know romance from friendship.

Will guided her along the aisles toward the ice-cream stand, but before they reached it, he stopped by a table of handmade knitted items.

"Can I help you, Will?" the woman asked as he plowed through the scarves.

"I'm looking for a red one."

She laid down her knitting needles and leaned below the table. When she straightened, she held a bright red scarf. "Like this?"

"Perfect," he said. "I'll take it."

She watched him pay the woman, and when she slipped it into a plastic grocery bag, he turned and handed it to Christine.

"For me?"

"To match your red gloves."

She grinned at his endearing expression. "But it's not even Christmas."

"It's always Christmas in my heart," he said, steering her to the back of the building where ice-cream chairs and tables had been placed.

Christine stared at the plastic bag, touched by the unexpected gift. So many of her experiences on the island had been unexpected. "Thanks. You're too good to me."

As they walked, she couldn't help but compare him to other men she knew—men at her office and men who lived in her apartment building. Some were nice, but they either seemed patronizing or pushy or with a goal in mind—a goal she didn't share.

At the stand, she and Will designed their sundaes, amid others in line who knew Will's name and soon learned hers.

When they'd settled at the table, her thoughts moved from Will's charm to her business ideas.

"How do you like the bazaar?" he asked, dipping into the mixture of ice cream, syrups, cherries, nuts and sprinkles topped with whipped cream.

"Fun. Different. Life here seems easy. Not easy really, because things like shopping and dentist appointments are more complicated, but easygoing. Sort of cozy."

He gave that some thought. "It's definitely close-knit and friendly."

"I can see that," she said, eager to move along to another topic. "I wanted to talk to you about those ideas I mentioned."

"Jewelry ideas?" Concern settled on his face.

"All your products. I'm just curious if you do marketing and promotion?"

He laughed. "We have an automatic market when the tourists arrive. They hit every shop on Main Street and Market. It's what they do."

"But after tourist season? What then?"

He slipped his hand over hers and gave it a pat. "Then we get cozy."

Cozy. The word came back to bite her. Apparently Will didn't have her drive for success. She imagined he could double his income, triple it, maybe, with Internet marketing. Items handcrafted on the island would automatically have a draw. Before she could speak her mind, Will spoke.

"Talking about business. Tell me about Creative… What's it called again?"

"Creative Productions. We develop marketing strategies and create commercial advertising for different venues—TV, radio, newspaper, magazines— you get it."

"Sounds challenging. How long have you been there?"

"Twelve years or so. I worked at Commercial Design for about three years out of college."

A look came over him that Christine couldn't read.

Will delved into his sundae and the conversation faded. He hadn't seemed interested in hearing her ideas and he certainly didn't like something she'd said about her work.

"I'd better get back to the booth," he said.

His abruptness startled her. "I need to get Grandma home, too." Yet she faltered, not wanting to leave with the tension she sensed between them. "I'll walk with you to the booth so I can—"

"I have much more at the studio. I think that's better."

She wasn't sure what he meant by that. Was it better she buy her gifts another time or was it better she leave? Hurt by his behavior, she clutched her gift to her chest. "I'll head over to Grandma then."

"See you later." He gave her a quick wave and walked away.

She stood a moment trying to collect herself and to hold back tears that threatened to sneak from behind her eyes.

Will kept moving forward. He wanted to turn back and look at her, but he couldn't. He felt like a heel, pushing her away like that, but she'd thrown him a curve when she answered his question.

His addition was good. Twelve years and three years equaled fifteen. She'd gotten out of college at least fifteen years ago. Fifteen years ago he'd been a freshman in high school. Will didn't care, but he feared Christine would. They'd become friends, and they'd just begun to have fun together. Once she realized his age—and she would—it was all over, and he knew it.

Someone grabbed his arm and, when he turned, Jude stood beside him with a grin on his face.

"So that's the chick you were telling me about," he said.

Will drew back. Chick? He'd never considered Christine a chick. "She's the *woman*," he said, hoping to make a point.

"She's not bad at all," Jude said. "So how's it going?"

"Good. Sales are better than last year, I think."

Jude punched his shoulder. "Not the sales. I mean with her. How's that going?"

"Fine. We've come to an amiable agreement. As long as she's here, we can tolerate each other, I think."

"Tolerate? Dude, where are your eyes? That lady's a better prize than that new sled outside Doud's."

"Do you want me to put in a good word for you, Jude?"

"Would you?" His eyes widened.

"No. And remember that."

Jude drew back and held up his hand. "I'm only kidding, Will. You said you're not interested, but apparently I have that wrong. Sorry, man."

Will opened his mouth to rebut, but nothing came. He was interested in Christine. Why try to pretend he wasn't? "It's okay," Will said, extending his hand.

"Sure, man," Jude said, giving him a curious look. He rattled on about the restaurant and Doud's sled, but Will's mind had stopped at his own admission.

He liked Christine, and he feared his feelings had headed off in directions he couldn't control. He barely knew the woman, but he sensed a pull that only God could cause. The attraction made no sense to him.

Chapter Eight

"Chet, you know I'd be back if I could. I didn't tell my mom to break her hip."

She listened to his superior attitude, and she controlled herself from knocking it down a peg. She had the ammunition, but she thought better of it. If she reminded him of his underhanded ways with her, she'd only put herself in a deeper hole.

"Look, Chet, think compassion. Can you do that?"

"What's that?" he asked her.

She wanted to give a smart remark back. "I don't know what you expect me to do. I'm all my parents have, and they—"

He cut her off and his question struck her.

"Yes, I have a brother, but he's married and lives out of state. My dad—"

She cringed at his next demand. "Look, I have two more weeks' vacation." Her vacation. Her stomach knotted. This wasn't the way she wanted to spend her vacation, but Chet wasn't going to manipulate her. "That'll nearly take me to the Christmas holidays. She's improving every day. Maybe by then, I'll—"

Chet's demand charged through her as he cut her off.

Her hopes fell to the ground. "I realize I have clients and yes, I'm going to talk with them today. I'll work out something about the meeting."

Christine hung up and fell backward on her bed. Tears slipped from the corners of her eyes and dripped to the quilt beneath her. Chet had made the threats she'd expected. She could go over his head, but it could destroy her. Right now, she needed to keep things low-key and try to cooperate as best she could.

She'd forgotten about a meeting she had with a client in less than a week, a big client who needed a sizable ad campaign. She wasn't the type to forget, but she wouldn't dwell on this now. She'd promised them mountains, and she'd better get busy. If she couldn't keep her appointments, someone else could. She'd be slipping from her status at the company.

As the outcomes swirled in her head, she pushed the heels of her hands against her eyes to stop the welling of tears. She refused to feel sorry for herself.

She rose and slid forward, her feet dangling from the mattress. Since she'd been here, she'd learned to enjoy some things about being laid-back—*cozy,* as she'd called it a couple days earlier. But it was more than cozy. The world had a sense of calmness and acceptance. Life had stresses, but they were different. They lacked the panic and the tension that she'd come to accept in her work and in city life.

She recalled the traffic jams on Southfield Road and I-696. She'd line up for miles. Her time would be frittered away while she directed her anger at drivers cutting her off and driving down the shoulder to sneak in ahead of her.

But here on the island, traffic? She smiled. Traffic was two horses and a carriage or two snowmobiles passing on a quiet road. She found something about that image soothing. No wonder her grandmother still looked so good even after her stroke. A little droopy in the face, perhaps, but she still had a sparkle in her eyes and a will to live fully.

Christine's thoughts slipped back to Will. She still felt troubled about what had happened at the bazaar. Yesterday he'd been busy at the event, too, and they hadn't really talked. Today he'd slipped away without a hello or goodbye. She longed to know what she'd done.

She pictured Will in the studio—his confidence and sense of being, sense of control. She admired his creativity, and though she was certain he had deadlines and responsibilities, he could pace himself. He could say yes or no to a job. He could take a day off without having his director threaten him. He could come home early and go in late if the fancy struck him.

She lowered her head in her hands. She'd been so excited to tell him about her great ideas for his store, and now she felt depressed and miserable. Being upset solved no problems. She'd find an answer.

Christine forced herself to rise. She dabbed powder around her eyes to cover the redness. The last thing she wanted was for her grandmother to know she had become upset again. Her grandmother mentioned a couple of the circle ladies were bringing her some jigsaw puzzles after her therapy. Christine hoped she could take the snowmobile—she looked to heaven and begged for mercy—and drop by the studio. She had to find out what was wrong.

Will lifted his head from his work, and his breath left him. Christine stood in the doorway of the studio, a smile on her face, but her eyes were questioning. What could he tell her? Not the truth. First he needed to figure out what he wanted and where he wanted this to go.

"Hi," he said, trying to remove the apprehension from his voice. "What brings you here?"

"Christmas gifts. You told me to drop by, and Grandma Summers has company."

"Great," he said, before pausing to ask his next question. "How did you get here?"

"The sled. You give good lessons."

That made him grin. "Thanks."

"How was the bazaar on Sunday?"

"Just about as busy as Saturday."

"Who won Doud's sled?"

He shrugged. "A year-round resident."

"Oh," she said. "Then it wasn't me."

"No, it wasn't you." He knew they were batting around the inevitable, so he took a different tack. "Sorry about Saturday. I didn't mean to let my mood affect our fun."

She drew closer, resting her hand against a display case. "What was that all about? I figured I did something, but I didn't know what."

"It was me," he said, feeling less than capable.

"What?" Her eyes narrowed as if his response had confused her.

"You're so sure of yourself in business. You have tremendous drive. I've seen it since you've gotten here. Your mind never stops."

She drew back. "It comes across that much?"

He shrugged. "I'm not saying it's bad, but I know you're anxious to get back to your work, and I—I'm not as anxious to have you go."

She studied his face. "I've been a diversion, I know."

"Diversion? Christine, you're more than a diversion. I really like you. You're great to be with. You make me laugh. I—"

"And somewhere in there I make you feel less confident and less capable. That doesn't make sense. You should want me to leave."

"It's difficult to explain. The longer you've been here, the more you've let down your…" He struggled for the words. "You've let go of your job at times. I see the love you have for your grandmother despite your drive to get back to work. You—"

"I know."

He felt his eyes widen at her admission.

"You look surprised that I see that in me, but I do. Let me tell you what happened today. I called my boss."

He listened while she told him her plight. He had to admit she'd fought a good fight. The vacation days were the biggest evidence. She'd once said she didn't want to give those up. "What will you do?"

She lowered her head and shook it. "I don't know. I'll do what I can and pray that Grandma Summers improves enough for me to go back when the time comes. Or…"

Her voice faded, but he wanted to know more. "Sounds as if your boss is trying to get even for some reason. Do you know why?"

She shook her head. "I really don't want to talk about it today. I need to decide what I can do. There are clients I need to talk with, and I may have to go back to the office for a day or so this week." She lowered her head again, then lifted it. "I hate to ask you but—"

"If you need me, Linda and I can handle it. I'm sure."

"Really?"

"We handled it a couple days before you got here, and your grandmother is doing better now."

"Thanks, Will. I feel much better with your offer. I can't tell you how much."

"I have some news," he said, the words blurting from him more loudly than he expected. He noticed the surprised look on Christine's face.

A frown wrinkled her forehead. "What kind of news?"

"My parents are coming up on the weekend for an early Christmas."

Her expression showed her confusion. "That's good news, isn't it?"

"Right," he said, trying to convince himself.

"Why early?"

"They have their Christmas traditions, and I said I couldn't get there this year so they're coming here."

She fell quiet, as if trying to understand. "Are you worried about Grandma Summers? Is that why you're not going home?"

"That's a small part of it." He turned away, afraid to look into her eyes for fear she'd read the truth. "I don't enjoy the family's social calendar. They either drag me with them—not always happy about it because I don't have the proper clothes—or I stay with the family and wish I were here." He finally looked at her.

She became quiet again, her eyes shifting from him to the distance. "I look forward to meeting them."

Her comment twisted in his stomach. "Say that after the fact." He heard the bitterness in his voice, and he regretted letting her see it.

He steadied himself. "Ready to look around for your gifts? I always give my friends a great bargain."

She gave him a pleasant look, but her voice seemed strained. "My credit card is ready. Show me the way."

* * *

Christine lowered her cell phone and pulled back her shoulders. Done. She had to go back tomorrow for an overnight stay. She'd hinted at changing the appointment, but her client hadn't been receptive to change, and she knew if she wanted to keep the company happy, she'd better make the trip.

Flying from the Pellston Regional Airport to Detroit Metro, then renting a car seemed easier than driving the five hours home. She checked the flight schedule. The trip flying would take about an hour and twenty minutes. She could even fly back to the island the same day, but she wouldn't. She wanted to see her mother while she was there.

Christine rubbed the gritty feeling from her eyes. She hadn't slept well. All night, she'd waded through the subliminal undertones of Will's reasons to stay on the island for Christmas. Bitterness seemed to rise from the mix of emotions she sensed in him— bitterness and disapproval. His attitude made her curious, and she was anxious to meet his parents.

When he'd suggested she look at his stock, she'd been relieved. It had distracted her from speculating.

Will's talent amazed her. The beadwork had been lovely, and he'd promised her a lesson. He told her bead making was simple, but that would seem the same as her telling him planning an advertising campaign was easy. It could be when the person had expertise.

She'd purchased a number of items to use as Christmas gifts—a gorgeous molded plate made with crushed glass for her mother. Will called it frits—a whole new language for her. She selected a string of beads in shades of blue for her sister-in-law, stained-glass barrettes for her two nieces, and a butterfly sun catcher for her coworker Sandy. She'd admired one for herself but let it pass. She'd spent enough money, and she still had numerous gifts to buy. Perhaps if she could spare a few hours, she could shop in the Detroit area when she went home.

Home. She pictured her loft in Royal Oak, looking over the store-front business area. The only trees were in the distance, appearing over housetops. She liked her place, but lately the image of the wide-open space seemed stark and empty. It wasn't like her grandmother's house, with doors sprawling along hallways, nooks and crannies and rooms she hadn't used in years.

With her decision made, Christine headed to the first floor. She stood in the doorway watching Judy encourage her grandmother to lift her arms and legs. The progress seemed slow but steady, and that gave Christine hope.

"How's it going?" Christine asked as she sat nearby. "You're using the sofa today."

"It's lower and firmer," Judy said. "It adds to the challenge, but I can see an improvement."

She turned to Christine. "You know, the insurance only covers three more weeks. That gets you up to Christmas. I hope you or someone can continue the therapy here, rather than sending her—"

"We'll work something out," Christine said, stopping the woman from suggesting they send her grandmother to an assisted-living complex. She'd seen the look in her grandma's eyes. She couldn't do that to her.

"Grandma." Christine faltered. "I'm going to have to go home for a couple of days—I need to get online and make my reservations—but Will said he and Linda could stay with you while I'm gone."

"We'll do fine. Don't worry."

Her grandmother said the words, but Christine saw a look of concern on her face.

"I promise I'll be back. I'm planning an overnight visit home—Wednesday, I think, and I'll be back Thursday evening."

"I know this is a hardship for you," her grandmother said. "If I could make it any different—"

"Grandma, don't say that. We'll talk later." She patted her grandmother's hand and headed upstairs to her cell. She needed to make reservations for the flight and car, then tell her father she was coming for a brief visit, and while she was at it, she wanted to make lunch plans with her friend, Ellene, and see how married life had affected her.

When Christine came down the stairs, she found her grandmother in the living room, her Bible in her hands.

She waited a moment before Ella looked up from her reading. "Judy said you're doing well."

"That's what she said."

Christine sat across from her grandmother. "I made plans, and I called Linda. She's ready to come in to help you in the morning and get your meals, and when she can't be here, Will said he has no problem getting home early."

"I know. I'm frustrated, I guess, and when that happens, I seek God's Word. I always find comfort in this book." She rested her hands on the Bible.

Christine leaned back, ready to be open with her grandmother. "When I came here, I'd been drifting from church attendance. The last two Sundays have been nice being with you in church. I love the hymns, and the lessons haven't hurt me, either."

Her grandmother only looked at her.

"I'm sure you didn't know but—"

"But I did." A faint, lopsided grin settled on her face.

"You did?"

"You can't fool an old lady, Christine. I knew you didn't want to go to church, and I could tell from your attitude that you'd drifted a little too far from the Lord, but I see the difference, and it does my heart good."

"But I didn't say anything." She searched her grandmother's face.

"No, but I saw it in your manner. Actions speak louder than words. I know you've heard that a thousand times, but it's true."

Christine hung her head. She remembered saying the same. "Faith without positive action was a dying faith."

"But remember that we're saved by grace alone,

and not good works. The Bible tells us that, but when the Lord has blessed us, then we want to show our love by doing as He would want. Those are the things that everyone can see."

A smile pulled at Christine's mouth. "I remember a song I sang in the teen group years ago—"They Will Know We Are Christians By Our Love."

"I remember that song." She shifted the Bible and fondled the page. "It reminds us of our behavior. Since the stroke, I can't do as much, and I get frustrated with my fumbling arms and a leg that either stays glued to the floor or tries to trip me up."

"But you're getting much better now."

"I am, and I'm still filled with self-pity, but lately when that happens, I read from Psalms because they are a beautiful blend of prayer and praise.

"When I feel sorry for myself, I think of what could have happened with my stroke, and then I'm filled with thankfulness. Here's what I just read. It's from Psalms 142:3. 'When my spirit grows faint within me, it is You who know my way.'" She drew her attention from the scripture. "This verse is for you, too."

The verse wrapped around Christine's heart. She'd always struggled to find her own way, forgetting to ask God to guide her.

"And speaking of seeing change," her grandmother said. "In the past week, you glow. You're not like you were the day you came. I know you're still feeling stressed from your work, but you're not as determined—aggressive." She nailed Christine with her gaze. "You were aggressive when you arrived, but you've softened. You're a lovely woman, and now it shows."

Tears grew behind Christine's eyes. She had no idea she'd appeared aggressive to her grandmother. She opened her mouth to apologize, but she choked on the words.

"Don't be upset," her grandmother said. "You did nothing wrong, but now I see you and Will laughing about things. You're going off on the sled and coming back with rosy cheeks and a vibrance I haven't seen in you for years. The island can get in your heart and change you."

Had it been the island or her grandmother's love? And Will. He'd impacted her, too, by making her face herself. She pressed her hand against her chest, feeling the beat of her heart and the rise and fall of her lungs. She felt alive on the island, much more alive than she had at home.

"I love you, Grandma," she said. She rose and kissed the elderly woman's soft cheek.

"And I love you, too, Christine—more and more each day. I'll miss you when you go back home, and I know you must. I don't mean for this little trip, but later when I'm doing well. You've been good for me."

"You've been even better for me." She clasped her hand. "And now, let's work on the jigsaw puzzle. We need to get those fingers moving."

Chapter Nine

Will rose from the fireplace and waited a moment to see if the kindling caught the flame. When he was satisfied, he moved to the sofa, mesmerized by the fire sparking inside the hearth.

"That looks nice," Christine said, coming into the room. "Grandma decided to go to bed early. A couple of ladies from her circle are coming over to visit tomorrow."

She stepped past him heading for a chair, but Will reached out and pulled her down beside him. "The view's better from here."

Christine gave him a curious glance, then watched the flames licking along the log and settled back.

Will hunkered down beside her. "I'm glad people are beginning to treat her as if she's going to live. I know they mean well, but sometimes they only called or dropped off food, and they didn't stay. She misses her normal relationship with them."

"I know it's been hard on her."

"I suppose it has on you, too, missing your friends." A questioning tone accentuated his voice.

Her head lifted from the cushion. "That's funny."

"What?"

Her expression shifted from awareness to surprise. "I don't miss my friends, because I don't have many."

"You don't?"

"Not really. My life has been so filled with work that I come home exhausted and don't really socialize much."

"You must do something. Even I hang around with a few people."

"I have a good friend who moved when she got married, and I'm hoping to see her when I go to Detroit on Wednesday. I'll call her and see if we can meet for lunch or dinner."

"She's married?"

"Yes, I was her maid of honor. She's younger than I am, but we've been like sisters."

The reference to her age caught him again, and he struggled to keep from reacting. He needed to talk with her about that, but he feared if she knew the truth, she'd not give them a chance. Chance? He had a fleeting chance as it was. The woman lived near Detroit. He lived three hundred miles away on an island. That situation could undo any chance in itself.

"You're quiet," she said, leaning her head back again.

He turned to her, watching the firelight dance

across her face. The golden glow glinted in her hair, and her eyes sparkled even more brightly. "If you lived on the island, you'd have a good friend."

Will cringed hearing his inane comment, like a lovesick puppy. He expected her to laugh, but she didn't.

"I know. Grandma and I had a talk today about change. She thinks I've changed since I've come here."

The urge to touch her hair tangled his thoughts. He fought the desire until he couldn't control it any longer. He eased his finger upward and brushed a lock from her cheek. "You have. I've seen it, and I like it."

She didn't flinch as he swept the spun gold from her face. "You look worn-out."

"It's the trip. I hate leaving and dumping this on you and Linda. I'll be back the next day, but it's asking a lot."

He motioned to his shoulder and drew her head toward it. Her gaze drifted to his hand, and as she shifted closer, he slid his arm around her shoulders. "I wouldn't have volunteered if I hadn't wanted to help. I love your grandmother."

Christine lifted her head, and he wanted to kick himself for making a statement that caused her to shift away.

She looked at him closely. "I know you do, and that's another thing I couldn't understand. When I first met you, I thought you had an ulterior motive."

"Ulterior motive?" She'd thrown him with the comment. "What do you mean?"

"I don't know. I couldn't understand a man being so accommodating to an elderly woman without wanting something."

"Like what?"

"Like her money."

"Her money? I didn't know she had any money. That wouldn't have entered my mind." Now he'd straightened up and removed his arm from around her.

"You see, that was my bad attitude. I'm really sorry."

She fell against the cushion, and Will took advantage of her upset to embrace her again and draw her closer. "I hope you know—"

"My grandmother was shocked that I'd even said it."

"You told your grandmother?"

"She put me in my place. She talked about Christian love and compassion. That's something I lack so much."

He nestled his head against hers again. "Not anymore. You're willing to fight your boss for time to spend with your grandmother. That's not the action of someone who's not caring. I see your love every day that you're standing over her forcing her to do her therapy or encouraging her to work on the jigsaw."

"And it feels good." She turned toward him, her mouth so close to his he could feel her breath against his lips. "I've never imagined that helping someone could give me such a sense of purpose and—" she shrugged "—I don't know, happiness, I guess."

"It's because it happens right here." He lifted her hand and pressed it against his heart. "When things affect you here, instead of up there—" he used his free hand to motion to his head "—then it's a special gift. It's what God wants us to do, because we're doing it for Him."

A tender look moved to her face. "It's that Christmas heart you talked about." She snuggled closer, and he ran his finger over the soft flesh of her arm.

In the quiet, he listened to the snap of the log in the fireplace and watched the ash sprinkle down like glowing confetti.

"You'll be back Thursday," he said, breaking the silence.

"Probably around four in the afternoon. My meeting is in the morning, and I hope to leave after lunch."

"If we can get someone to stay with Grandma Ella, would you like to help me pick out a Christmas tree?"

"So early?"

"My folks will be here Saturday afternoon, and—"

Christine shifted. "Yes, that's a good idea. I forgot they were coming so soon. We want the house to look like Christmas."

"Just a little one for my place," he said.

"No, we'll put one up here, too. They'll come to dinner. You shouldn't just take them to a restaurant or feed them a microwave frozen dinner."

He chuckled. "I suppose you're right."

"We'll make a holiday meal. This will be fun."

He didn't want to destroy her plans, but nothing was very much fun with his family—unless Christine could work a miracle on them, and even God hadn't done that.

* * *

Christine stood at the car rental checking the time. She'd agreed to meet Ellene for lunch and a little shopping before she headed for the office. She decided to work on the project in the evening after most everyone had gone. The building would be quieter, and she wouldn't be distracted by co-workers dropping in to find out how she'd fared on the island. Later she would visit her parents. She missed them.

"Here you go," the clerk said, slipping her the paperwork. "Go through that door on the left, and they'll direct you to your car."

"Thanks," Christine said, picking up her overnight bag and following the clerk's directions.

Once she pulled away from Detroit Metro airport, she headed east on I-94. The pavement was dry with no signs of snow, but the barren trees and gray sky told her that winter was not far-off.

Traffic sped along on the highway, and she followed the signs and veered onto the Southfield Freeway merging with traffic. The familiar landmarks whipped past her window and left her feeling lonely. She pictured her grandmother doing her exercises—the laps they'd gotten to enjoy as they talked while pacing the familiar path through the house. Her grandmother seemed stronger every day.

And Will. His smile filled her mind and his silly humor that she'd grown to love. She knew he had problems, but he carried them well, not like the burdens she lugged around so often—her fears of falling short on her job, the competition that kept her awake at night—but for a short while, that had changed.

The freeway merged into a regular road, and she braked for the stoplight. She'd be on time, she noted, glancing at her watch. As she approached Ten Mile Road, the restaurant sign caught her eye—Wing Hong. She liked Chinese food and so did Ellene, and the restaurant wasn't noisy like so many were at lunchtime.

She pulled into the parking lot and entered the restaurant lobby. When she looked into the dining area with its red-and-black Asian decor, she saw Ellene's bright smile. She waved, and Christine hurried forward, her arms open.

"It's so good to see you," she said, grasping her friend to her chest. "I hope you didn't wait long."

"I was just seated," she said, holding Christine back and eyeing her from all directions. "What's up with you? You look better than I've seen you in so long. Something must agree with you up there."

Christine shrugged. "It's been a battle, but I'm surviving." She pulled off her coat, threw it on the bench and slipped into the booth.

"If it were a battle, you've come out the victor. You have the brightest glow, Christine, even more than when we spent an hour at the gym. I'm telling you, it must be the fresh air."

Christine laughed. "Can you picture me driving a snowmobile?"

Ellene shook her head. "You're kidding. Is that your only transportation?"

"Now with the snow. I didn't know what I was doing until Will gave me a lesson. I was so determined—"

Ellene grabbed her arm. "Hold on. Will? Who's Will?"

Christine tried to keep her voice calm, but she longed to talk about him. "He's my grandmother's boarder."

"Really?"

She studied Christine, and her scrutiny made Christine uneasy. "Really. I didn't know she had a boarder until he met me at the ferry depot."

"On a white steed?"

"No, with a taxi—horse and carriage no less."

Ellene grasped her hand and squeezed. "Please tell me. Something's going on, and I'm so excited for you. You like him, right?"

"I didn't want to, but I do, Ellene, and it makes no sense. I barely know him, and yet I feel I've known him forever. I was very edgy at first, but I came to my senses."

"Edgy?"

Christine told her how she'd worried about Will's motives, her jealousy with his closeness to her grandmother, and his island know-it-all. "But that's changed. He owns a business, and I have so many ideas for him."

"Is he open to that? You know a man and his business. If you interfere—"

"You order?" the Asian woman asked.

"I haven't looked." Christine flipped open the menu and gave it a quick scan. "I'll take the number six luncheon plate with wonton soup."

The waitress nodded, and after Ellene placed her order, the woman left.

"I mentioned ideas to him, and he didn't say anything." Or did he? Was that one of his silent moments?

"I don't mean to interfere, but I know how you are about business. You have set ideas, and they don't always work for someone else."

Christine was taken aback. "Do you really think I'm pushy?" *Aggresive.* Her grandmother's word made her wince.

"I didn't say pushy exactly. Your ideas are strong and you think they're right."

Was that so bad? Christine pondered what Ellene had said for a moment. "I do know a lot about marketing and that's where Will's business is weak. I think the Internet could be a boon to making him a—"

"Success?" Ellene frowned. "Do you think a man wants to hear you don't consider him a success? You know I did that to Connor, and it almost ruined our relationship. I don't want to see you ruin something before it has a chance to succeed."

"He knows I admire him."

"You say you admire him, but what you do really tells the tale." She brushed the air with her hand.

"Look. Ignore me. It's none of my business. Just tell me about him."

Christine let her friend's comments slide, but they stuck in the back of her mind as she told her about Will. Ellene's smile was as broad as her own when she talked about the sled lessons and the conversations in front of the fireplace. "I like him a lot, but it's sad."

"Sad?"

"Because I live here, and he lives there. He'd never come back to the city. I would stake my job on it."

"That's a pretty strong comment."

They paused while the waitress brought their soup and egg roll with a pot of Chinese tea.

"You'd have to meet him. The island has made a mark on him—a good mark. He belongs there. Remember how you felt about Harsens Island and how much Connor loved it."

"He still does, and guess what—so do I now that I'm there. Caitlin is so happy, too." She took a spoonful of soup. "I'd love to meet Will, but obviously that's not possible."

"I know, but wouldn't it be nice."

The conversation drifted to Ellene's construction business, her husband Connor's new sports store, and the reason Christine had come to town, but her thoughts clung to things Ellene had said. Her grandmother had talked about her aggressiveness, and now her friend had called her pushy and interfering.

Was that really how she'd acted?

* * *

"It's quiet here without Christine."

Will turned his head and looked at Grandma Ella. "I was thinking that, too. Funny how a person can get used to scratchy long johns." He chuckled, and so did Grandma Ella.

"She did come across as a little abrasive around the edges, didn't she? But not anymore."

"She has you to thank for that," Will said, helping Ella with her laps. "It's great to see you on a cane."

"It's good to be on it. You can throw that walker into the garbage as far as I'm concerned."

He chuckled.

"I think two things made a difference in Christine's life," Ella said. "You and the Lord."

Will faltered. "Me? I didn't do a thing but teach her how to drive a sled."

"That was part of it. She got a taste of life on the island, and the Lord did the rest."

"But you were the catalyst."

Ella chuckled. "I did get her to church and shared some Bible verses with her, and she was open to that. Christine came here with a lot of guilt, and it's fading fast like the evening sun."

Will thought about what she'd said. Christine had arrived with a frown on her face and a negative attitude. They had faded until now he saw a radiant woman who'd discovered a lighthearted way of looking at things…at least most of the time.

"You've fallen in love with her."

Will tripped over his foot. "I what?"

"You can't hide it, Will. You're like a kid with a gift you've wanted forever, like a teenager with car keys. You can't get your fill of her. When my son, who's been gone a long time now, passed his driving test and got his license, he'd run to the grocery store at the drop of a hat."

"On the island?"

"No." She grinned. "When I lived in Detroit. I moved here when the house was left to me by my parents."

"I didn't know that."

"Lots of things you don't know." She gave him a wink. "But some things I do know, and you're in love."

"And I can't do a thing about it, Grandma Ella. Christine is a big-city girl. She has a job she loves, and a home in Royal Oak. I can't compete with that."

"Oh, Will, love doesn't compete. Hand me my Bible, and I'll tell you about love in First Corinthians."

"I know," he said. "Love is kind. It doesn't boast. It isn't rude. Love never fails. It protects. It doesn't envy. I know I forgot some."

"The most important. Love is patient. Give it time, Will, and pray about it. Nothing would make me happier than you and Christine finding a love that's blessed. But be patient. She's made long strides, but she'll stumble. It's part of her, but she's grown and that's been God's doing."

Love is patient. Will grasped on to that thought. Grandma Ella knew about life and the Lord. He'd trust her to give him good advice, and he trusted God to answer his prayers.

"So how did it go?"

Christine's head shot upward and she frowned. "Very well, Chet. Thanks."

He sauntered into her office and sat on the edge of her desk. "Is the deal set, then?"

"No, but it's close. They'll look it over and take it to their board meeting, but they sounded pleased with the presentation. They said they'd be in touch by tomorrow. I asked them to e-mail, since I won't be here."

He stood and put his hands on the desk, his face thrusting closer to hers. "You can't be a long-distance employee, Christine. I know you think you have all the good ideas, but we have others here who can do your job."

She rose and pushed back her chair. "Listen, Chet. You thought I had great ideas once. Remember?" She narrowed her eyes, hoping to nail him to the spot.

Instead he laughed. "That was a long time ago, Christine." He moved closer. "When you were gullible. You should have known better than to listen to my promises."

"That's water under the bridge, Chet. I'm not afraid of you, but I want to do my job here. People have problems sometimes—illness, emergencies—and I have one of those. I'm the only person available to help my grandmother. I'll take my two weeks' vacation. In fact I put in for that already, and it was approved."

"Really, and what about the Dorset project? Can you handle that long-distance?"

"If I must, I will."

"We'll see about that. You have to be ready in January. I'm thinking your team needs another leader."

"They'll be fine without me physically present. I'm in contact by e-mail and on the phone. I haven't died, Chet. I'm just a few miles away."

He grabbed the calendar from his desk. "Let's see. Those two weeks' vacation should take you to December fifteenth. We'll see you back here on December eighteenth then. You'll be home for Christmas."

Christine managed to hide her frustration. She needed longer, and she'd get it somehow. She'd looked forward to Christmas on the island.

Chet's smirk eroded her patience, and an idea came from nowhere. "FMLA, Chet, you've heard of FMLA, right? Family Medical Leave Act. I'm entitled to that. Twelve weeks of it, if I must. That's not what I want, but if I'm needed, that's what I'll have to do."

"We'll see about that, my friend. I've already told the big guy upstairs that I had to help you with the Emerson project since you were on vacation."

Her pulse escalated. "You out and out lied?"

"No, I did talk to them on the phone and said the meeting was set for today. I did help you, didn't I?"

He spun on his heel and vanished around the corner.

Christine sank into her chair and lowered her face into her hands.

Chapter Ten

Will grabbed the phone on the second ring.

"I'm back."

Christine's voice bubbled over the line, and Will felt a smile grow on his face. "How was it?"

"Pretty good. I had a nice visit with my friend over Chinese food, my mom seemed fine despite her hip, and the meeting with the client went well, I think."

"Then why only pretty good?"

She hesitated before she spoke. "It's a long story. I'll tell you later."

"Are you going with me to pick out the Christmas trees?"

"Where is the lot?"

"Down by the Chamber Riding Stables on Market and Cadotte. The junior class sponsors the tree sale."

"Sure, I'll go." He heard a pause. "But how do you get the tree back on the sled?"

He shook his head. "You have much to learn. In the sled's caboose or we can have it delivered."

"I do have a lot to learn."

Will heard another pause and wondered if her statement held more meaning than the reference to sleds.

"I picked up a couple things to add to the tree while I was shopping yesterday," she said.

"You've got my attention."

She laughed. "You'll have to wait. It's a surprise."

He loved the sound of her voice, and his chest grew tight, picturing her face. "I'll leave here shortly."

Will said goodbye and hung up, feeling as if he'd been given a gift by her call. He'd missed her so much while she was gone—only a day and a half, he knew, and the idea stressed him. What would he do when she left for good? Their relationship was like a shipboard romance, doomed to end when the boat docked at the final port.

He finished cutting the glass pieces he'd marked and closed the studio. A gloomy sky had lowered over the island the day before, reflecting the funk he'd been in, but it lingered today and didn't fit the mood he now felt.

Christine had returned, and the evening would be dedicated to Christmas—decorating the trees and listening to carols—and maybe having a cup of hot chocolate.

Will sped along the frozen earth, the snow forming a landscape of glass that glinted when the sun accidentally peeked from behind the clouds before it vanished again. The house appeared ahead, and he knew Christine was waiting inside.

She opened the door as he came up the walk.

"Ready?" he called. She held up her index finger, and in a moment, she darted outside dressed in her jacket and wearing the bright red scarf he'd bought to match her gloves.

He opened his arms, and she went into them. He teetered in surprise, yet thrilled to her candid action. It was what he'd wanted to happen.

"So tell me," he said, easing back. "Why was your time only pretty good?"

"It's Chet, my boss. He's pulling things on me again. He has a history of it. It's my fault. I fell for it one time, and once more he's manipulating things. I'll survive."

A gust caught them, and he saw her shiver. He noticed something more in her face, something that revealed the story was deeper and more serious than she wanted to admit.

"Let's go," he said, letting her climb onto the sled before he joined her.

While he waited, the lowering sun tried to peak from beneath the thick bank of clouds, but only a flicker lit the sky, then vanished again, leaving him with an unsettled feeling.

"It looks pretty," Christine said, standing back to admire her grandmother's tree. "I love these old Christmas balls."

"I was given some of them when I was a child," her grandmother said. "And many are from my mother's ornaments. They're antiques."

"And beautiful," Christine said. "These are the things we cherish about Christmas. It's not the gifts under the tree, but the memories—good memories."

Will drew closer to her and touched her shoulder. "I've never heard you so nostalgic."

"I know," she said, feeling his gentle touch shimmer down her arm. "Sometimes I amaze myself."

He grinned and gestured toward the foyer. "Let's tackle my tree. That won't take long, and then we'll have a treat."

"Don't worry if I'm not here when you come back in. I'm thinking of heading for bed."

Christine shifted to her side and rested her hand on her grandmother's arm. "Grandma, it's too early. Are you feeling all right?"

"I'm feeling wonderful, and you know what's the most special?"

Christine studied her face, wondering what she was about to say. "No."

"You calling me Grandma."

"I've always called you Grandma."

"No. I was Grandma Summers. It's nice just hearing the plain old Grandma. More loving, I think."

Christine's chest tightened. "I've always loved you, but now it's more personal, I guess."

"It's how we should be with Jesus," her grandmother said. "When we get personal is when He's our closest friend."

"I'll add a second to that," Will said.

The comments bounced around in Christine's thoughts. Had she ever had that kind of personal feeling about Jesus? Since she'd been on the island, she'd drawn closer.

"Ready?" Will asked, beckoning her to follow.

Christine bent and kissed her grandmother's cheek. "I love you."

Her grandmother's crepey hand pressed against hers. "I love you, too."

"I'll come back and check on you shortly." She gave a wave and followed Will into the foyer and through the back entrance leading to his apartment. Knowing her grandmother was within a few steps relieved the normal tension she felt when she was away, and Ella's getting steadier on the walker—even the cane—brought Christine joy. "Thank you, Lord." The praise lingered in her mind.

Will had already set his tabletop tree into a stand, and Christine waited while he dragged out a small box of decorations. She wasn't sure why he wanted his own tree. Yet as she watched the delight on his face—like a child on Christmas morning—she recognized the joy he had in preparing for Christmas.

"Help me untangle these," he said, pulling out a knotted string of miniature lights.

She shook her head at the task but took a section and began solving the puzzle. "This reminds me of my grandmother's jigsaw. I insist she use her left hand when I'm watching her. It's difficult, but she'll get there. I see the determination in her face."

Will reached across the space and brushed her cheek. "You're a very devoted granddaughter. It looks so good on you."

"Thanks. I'm enjoying the time with her, and I mean that. I can't help but worry about my job, but…"

He let the string of lights sag in his hand and gazed at her. "Tell me about this guy—your boss."

"Chet." She drew up her shoulders while frustration charged through her again. "You'll ruin my evening if you make me talk about him."

"Sorry, but I'd like to understand what you're going through."

"It's something I'm ashamed of, Will. I haven't told anyone, and it's been eating at me. I was gullible and naive. *Stupid* is an even better word."

He let the string drop to the ground and moved two steps toward her. He took the lights from her hand and drew her closer. "Whatever you did or said, it's easier to live with when it's out in the open."

She noticed his expression and suspected he also had things in his life he'd rather forget.

Christine looked into his eyes, and as his discomfort faded, she saw the same gentleness arise that she'd seen when he cared for her grandmother. Will's natural inclination toward compassion aroused her longing. She wished she had the same ability to put others first always.

He guided her to the sofa and motioned for her to sit. She wanted to pull away and to decorate the tree rather than bare her past—the embarrassing, disgusting truth of her gullibility.

Will didn't move, and she gave in and sat. She tried to hide her trembling hands, but Will noticed.

"When you say things aloud, Christine, it gets rid of them." He slipped his arm around her shoulders. "Tell me about Chet. Don't let the past spoil what we have."

Don't let the past spoil what we have. But what did they have? She knew what she longed for, but she also knew a relationship with Will was destined to failure. They were worlds apart, and the knowledge squeezed against her heart.

Yet she looked at his face, so open to hearing, and realized he'd offered her a gift. What difference did it make? If nothing were to become of their relationship, then she had nothing to lose except finally confessing her wrongdoing—a sin that had eaten at her for years and for which she'd already paid a depressing price.

She swallowed, then lowered her head to collect her thoughts. How had it all begun? "Chet was a new, upcoming man in the company when I met him. I'd joined the team a few months before he had." The words tasted bitter, and the acrid memory churned in her throat. "He flirted. I flirted. After a few weeks, we dated. He told me how much he admired my work. My ideas. Me."

Will shifted and rested his hand on her arm, his finger brushing along her skin.

"He started talking commitment. Life plans." She sorted her thoughts, trying to remember what had happened first. "He told me how good our lives would be if he became a top adman. He suggested I help him. We'd brainstorm, and he'd present the idea as his own." She turned to look at Will. "I'd become very respected when I joined the company. They said I had innovative ideas with a touch of wit."

"That doesn't surprise me," Will said. "I love your spunky attitude."

"Spunky?" She thought back and agreed she had been spunky with him from the beginning. "Chet wanted the top guns to think the ideas were his and not mine. He said it would be better for our relationship and our status as a couple."

"That's chauvinistic," Will said, the disapproval evident in his voice.

"But I was smitten. I fell for it. I was flattered and foolish. I gave him my best ideas, and he became their golden boy over the next few months."

"How could you do that? You're so strong."

"I am now. I wasn't then. But when I saw what was happening, I started to back away. I told him he was set, and I needed to show I had talent."

"What did he do?"

"He said he wanted to marry me." She swallowed again, feeling tears fill her eyes. "He said once we were married and settled, then it wouldn't matter. He would be my director. I'd be his wife, and he knew my talent."

"Slick move. Disgusting, but slick."

"That's not the worst. He knew me well." Christine swallowed back the revulsion that the memory evoked and wondered how Will would react. "Without a wedding or a wedding date, we became— became involved, and I felt trapped. He knew that I had a Christian upbringing and I had morals. If I revealed the truth, he could do the same. I felt sick."

Will released a deep groan, and she felt him flinch, but his finger kept its steady rhythm along her arm.

"When he was promoted with his own office, he suddenly lost interest. I realized I'd been duped, and I was disgusted with myself."

"Christine. I don't know what to say." He lowered his head and was quiet while she struggled with what he was thinking.

"I shouldn't have told you. I knew you'd think less of me."

"No, I don't. You were naive. Those are the reasons I didn't want to go into corporate business. I don't play games. I don't stab my friends in the back. I don't lie or use people."

"I know you don't, Will."

"Couldn't you do anything?"

"What? He had me in the middle. I'd make a fool of myself no matter what I did or said. First I'd have to admit what I'd done, and then, he could say it was all sour grapes. I felt trapped in my own sin."

"And now?"

"He's confident I still won't say anything. I'm

very respected. Once his promotion became solid, he didn't need to prove anything. He's the team director, and he knows I'll continue to work hard and give the company what they want—innovative ads with a unique twist."

"Why is he fighting you now? You'd think he'd be happy to have you on leave for a couple of months."

"It's control. It's cat and mouse. He loves the torment. He threatened my job."

"To fire you?"

"No. To give my clients to someone else to direct. I don't have much to stand on when I'm not there. It means struggling to get a foothold again when I get back. It's the principle of the thing, but I'm not going to sit back and take it. I have rights, and I'll go to the top if I must."

"I would expect nothing else. God knows the truth, Christine, and the truth will win out."

His words wove through her mind. Will's faith amazed her. She longed to understand. "Will, I really want to know—"

Before she finished the sentence, he'd risen and held his hands out to her. "We need to get this tree finished. It's late and my parents arrive tomorrow."

She glanced at her watch. Nearly ten o'clock. She rose, and he drew her into his arms and gave her a reassuring hug. She held her question and joined him in untangling the tree lights.

Lights led to the ornaments, and when he began hanging them, Christine darted from the room and found the surprises she'd purchased for him. When she returned, he was standing back and looking at the tabletop tree.

"Not bad," he said. "A little scanty, but that's okay. I'll enjoy your grandmother's more than this one."

"I can fill in a couple of gaps."

He gave her a tender look when he saw the two packages in her hand.

She extended the one. "This is probably silly, but I thought it was lovely."

Will took the bag and pulled out an orb wrapped in bubble wrap. "Why is it silly?" He peeled away the protective covering while the question hung in the air. When the ball appeared, he lifted it and held it to the light. "Christine, it's beautiful. This is handblown."

"I know, but you could probably make one yourself."

"What difference does that make? This was from you and that makes it special." He turned to eye the tree, and when he located a larger opening in the branches, he added a hook to the ornament and hung it there. The ball twirled below the limb, the light refracting in the swirls of color.

"It is pretty," she said, pleased that he really seemed to like it. She fingered the next package and felt color rising up her neck, wondering if she'd made a mistake with this gift. She prayed he didn't misunderstand.

"So what's in the other bag?" he asked.

"Don't laugh and don't embarrass me with this

one. I spotted it in the mall at one of those craft booths, and I couldn't resist. Please take it in the spirit it's given."

A questioning frown filled his face. She handed him the package. When he opened it, the frown shifted to a broad smile.

"I'm taking this in the spirit that I prefer. I hope you don't mind." He looked at her with eyes that made her melt. "I love it."

"I thought it would remind you of the photo you entered in the calendar contest."

"It reminds me of more than that."

She looked at the white handcrafted wooden heart personalized with their initials in red and the plus sign, just as they'd written it in the snow.

"This deserves a prominent spot," he said, moving an ornament to place the heart at the front of the tree. "And the gift deserves a real hug." He turned and opened his arms to her.

She stepped into his embrace, amazed at the feeling of comfort and familiarity that washed over her.

When she eased away, he urged her closer. "I bought a surprise, too," he said, reaching beneath the tree.

His hand reappeared from under the branches, and she caught her breath. A sprig of mistletoe hung between his fingers. His eyes captured hers as he raised the mistletoe above her head, his eyes asking if it was okay.

She couldn't respond, her own heart fighting for and against his action. They were spiraling even more deeply into a whirlwind relationship too fragile to withstand a gale.

He gathered her into his arms, his mouth finding hers. When she closed her eyes, her thoughts swirled like the colors of the lovely glass ornament. The gentle touch, the warmth that swept through Christine stunned her. His hand holding the mistletoe lowered to her back, nestling her closer as his mouth found hers again.

Reality smacked her. Why had she allowed this to happen? Sadness pried at the lovely liquid emotion that washed along her limbs. Nothing could undo their differences.

Will must have sensed her reserve, because he eased back, confusion spreading to his face. "What is it?"

She lowered her head. "Nothing you can fix."

"It's not the past, is it? I understand about that. Please, don't let those memories ruin what we have."

Ruin what we have? Again the words wove through her mind. "It's not that, Will." What did they have? A new friendship? Was it more? It couldn't be. "It's us. My work is downstate. Yours is here. I live in the city. You live on an island."

He rested his index finger on her lips. "Shush. I have no idea what this means, but God is in charge, and with Him all things are possible."

If God were in charge, He'd made a bungle of her life. She looked into Will's pleading eyes but couldn't tell him she disagreed. All things were not possible. She knew that for certain.

Chapter Eleven

When Christine heard Will calling her from the back hallway, she headed toward his voice.

He beckoned to her. "I want you to meet my parents." He appeared stressed even though he smiled.

"I'd like to meet them," she said, anxious to find out why their son had the negative feelings he seemed to have.

She walked through the doorway, then into his apartment. The couple was seated on the only two comfortable chairs in the crowded room. They looked out of place—his father in a dark business suit and his mother in a shirtwaist burgundy dress, her neck adorned with a string of pearls and her feet covered with fur-topped boots. They gave the illusion of a wealthy family dropping by to visit Tiny Tim at Christmas. The scene was paradoxical.

"This is Christine," Will said.

His parents studied her with suspicion in their

eyes, and sadly, the look took her back to her own scrutiny of Will when she came to the island.

"Hello," she said, moving forward to offer her hand.

His mother's fingers brushed hers, then his father gave a firmer handshake, but his eyes continued to probe questioningly.

"I'm Ella's granddaughter. Ella is Will's landlady, as you know."

Will's mother looked her over again. "And you live here, too."

Christine heard the insinuation in his mother's voice. "No. I'm from the Detroit area, as you are. I've been staying here to help with Ella's therapy until my parents can arrive." She saw their glazed look. "My mother broke her hip on a cruise. Will probably told you my grandmother had a stroke."

Will slid a kitchen chair behind her, and Christine sat as his mother's eyebrows lifted.

"No, he didn't," she said.

"That's a shame," Will's father said. "Will must be a burden on your grandmother."

Will opened his mouth but Christine cut him off, shocked at their comment. "Not at all. He's been very helpful." Her thoughts shot back to her criticism ·of Will's belongings scattered around her grandmother's house. The problem had faded in her eyes. She looked at Will, and he grinned back. She hoped his parents witnessed the friendship between them. One smiling face, at least, was needed among this scowling group.

Will pulled up an ottoman and sat beside the table holding the Christmas tree.

Mr. Lambert turned his attention to her. "So you're from the city."

Christine nodded.

"And what do you do there?"

"I'm in advertising. I work for Creative Productions."

He shot a look at Will. "You see, Will. This woman has a head on her shoulders."

"Dad, I—" Will let his comment drop with the shake of his head.

Christine's back stiffened. "Have you been to Will's studio? He's extremely talented."

"We'd hoped he would make glass his hobby," his mother said. "We'd had such expectations."

"It's not a hobby," Will blurted, "and we don't need to hear that again, Mom. I'm doing very well, and I know I've disappointed you."

"Will has a thriving business," Christine added, then turned to him. "You'll have to take them there."

Out of nowhere, she became uneasy with her involvement in their discussion, and changing the subject became her mission. "How was your trip?"

"Long," Mrs. Lambert said. "Too long. We should have flown."

Mr. Lambert gave her a fleeting frown, then redirected his focus. "You could have flown home for the holiday, Will. Your room is waiting for you."

His room? Christine flashed him a look. She no

longer had a room at home. Her mother turned it into a craft room—scrapbooking, sewing, needle-work—as each hobby caught her fancy.

Will let the comment roll off his shoulders. "I'm busy here. I have a number of projects that need to be completed for the holidays. My customers come first. I think you'd appreciate that motto."

Christine cut in to the conversation again, fearing it was heading for an argument. "Before you leave, my grandmother is looking forward to meeting you, and she'd like you to have some refreshments."

Mrs. Lambert's eyes flashed from Will to her husband and back as if she hadn't heard. "I thought you had a real apartment, Will."

He grinned. "This is a real apartment, but it's small and not set up for socializing. You'll have more room at Grandma Ella's."

His father grunted. "If you were in the business at home, Will, you'd be successful and have a home of your own. A large home."

"I'm happy here, Dad."

"You appear to be an older woman," Mrs. Lambert said, turning to Christine. "I suppose you have your own home."

Older woman? Christine flinched, wondering what she meant. She glanced around the room for a mirror. She'd thought she looked pretty good today. "I have a loft in Royal Oak. I like it there."

"One of those new lofts. They're very popular," Mr. Lambert said. "That's what you need, Will. Some space to call home, and that reminds me."

His father dug into his breast pocket and pulled out a checkbook. Christine's mouth gaped as she watched him scribble a check and tear it off the pad. He extended it to Will. "We didn't know what you needed so we thought you could use this."

Will took the check, glanced at it and handed it back. "Dad, I don't need this amount of money. I don't need anything."

His father flexed his palm to stop him. "No. I'm sure you have needs." The tone of his voice made the meaning clear. "You can find a real condo on the island." He turned to Christine. "You look like a bright woman. Can't you convince this boy to find an attractive condo to live in?"

Christine reeled with his comment. *This boy?* She looked at Will's manly profile and shook her head. "I have no influence on your son, Mr. Lambert. I think that's his decision."

Will laid the check in front of his father. "Thank you, Mom. Dad. I'm happy living here, and I have everything I need." He glanced toward Christine with a telling look. "Nearly everything I need."

She squirmed with discomfort, understanding his innuendo.

Will rose. "By the way, I have something for you." He disappeared into his bedroom.

They sat the seconds in silence, watching the doorway. Will returned with a large narrow box—one of his large stained-glass windows, Christine guessed.

"Merry Christmas," Will said, setting the gift in front of his parents.

His father eyed the carton.

Will lowered himself onto the ottoman. "I'm sorry, I didn't gift wrap it."

His father pulled the tape from the box, and when he struggled to withdraw the gift, Will rose to help him pull out the glass.

"Will, it's beautiful," Christine said, amazed that he'd never shown her the wonderful landscape—distant trees scattered along the rolling hills where a winding path led away into an amazing sunset.

His parents gaped, then passed each other looks as if they were pleasantly surprised.

"This is very lovely," his mother said. "I didn't know you worked with such large pieces of glass."

"I thought it could hang in the large window in the library or maybe the living room picture window. Whichever you prefer. I'll show you how to hang it before you leave."

His father studied the scene. "Now what would you get for something like this?"

"At least two or three hundred dollars," his mother said, looking at Will with question.

"I've sold similar for fourteen hundred dollars."

His mother's eyes widened. "Really?"

"Glass is priced by the square foot, the type of glass, and the complexity of the design." Will helped his father slide the piece back into the carton. "It's heavy, Dad. Would you prefer me to mail it home rather than your carrying it?"

"Mail it? No, it would cost you a fortune."

"I can afford to send it home."

His father shook his head. "I'll have them handle it at the ferry, and someone can help me get it into the car."

Will didn't ask again and rose. "You can leave your coats here. Why don't we go and have some refreshments with Grandma Ella?" Will motioned his parents toward the door.

Christine went on ahead, her mind rolling with what she'd observed and heard in their bouncing conversation. They treated Will as if he were a child, as if he didn't have a brain in his head. No wonder he had negative feelings about their visiting. The astounding relationship set her back. Why couldn't these people accept Will's decision to be a craftsman of such lovely artwork?

She led them to the doorway and paused to usher them in. Her grandmother sat in her favorite chair, a sweet smile on her face. She'd been anxious to meet Will's family, and Christine prayed the visit didn't disappoint her.

After her grandmother had been introduced, the Lamberts settled on the sofa, and Christine headed for the kitchen, puzzled about the difficult relationship Will had with his parents. They'd wanted to guide his life, and he'd rebelled. How could he honor his parents when he didn't think it was best for him?

Before she could fill the teapot, Will stood behind her.

"What can I do?" he asked, touching her shoulder.

Warmth swept down her arm. She turned, his lips

so close to hers, producing a strong desire to kiss away the sadness she saw in his eyes. "You can entertain your parents while I bring in the tray."

"They'll do better alone with Grandma Ella."

Christine didn't argue. "How about filling the coffee carafe while I get the teapot ready."

As she worked, she grinned, thinking they had their personal Mrs. Fields to supply them with unending cookies. The neighbor had brought over a new supply of homemade Christmas treats. She arranged the items on a plate, then loaded it all onto a tray.

"All set," she said, eyeing Will.

Though he smiled, his face looked strained.

She whisked past him into the living room, feeling him close behind. His familiar scent, citrus and spice, captured her senses.

"Here we are," Christine said, lowering the tray to the chest in front of the sofa. She managed to give Will's mother a pleasant look though tension snapped in the room.

Christine poured the coffee and tea, then offered the sugar and cream. She handed the Lamberts dessert plates, but they appeared to accept them as a social nicety rather than wanting to be social.

"We have room for you and Mrs. Lambert to stay here," Christine offered, doing it out of courtesy and not desire.

"Thank you, but we have a lovely room at the

Market Street Inn," Mrs. Lambert said. "It's near Main Street."

"That's very close to my store," Will said.

"We're sure having strangers in the house would be difficult for you." Will's father gestured toward him. "Even Will has overstayed his visit."

"Visit?" Ella's head bent back as if the comment had knocked her off balance. "Will's no guest here. He's like a grandson, and he's been very good company for me." Her gaze shifted to Will's as if she wondered if he'd said something to his parents. "I enjoy having him here, and I always thought he felt the same."

"I do, Grandma Ella. Don't worry about that."

Her shoulders eased. "He saved my life, you know." She began the long story about her stroke and Will's part in saving her. "You can see I think a great deal of your son."

"That's very nice," Mrs. Lambert said, "but shouldn't a young man have friends his own age?"

"Mother, I have friends of all ages." Irritation sparked in his voice for the first time. "My parents forget I'm not their teenager anymore."

"Sometimes, I wonder," his mother mumbled.

Mr. Lambert patted his wife's arm. "We would have preferred a different life for Will," Mr. Lambert said, looking at Ella.

"You're unhappy with Will's choices?" Ella asked as if she couldn't believe what she'd heard. "You can be very proud of your son. He's so talented, and he's a fine Christian man."

His father gave her a feeble grin. "We have standards in our family, and we had hoped our only son would follow in my footsteps."

Ella gave him a steady look. "When I was a young mother, I always wanted my children to have a life better than me, not the same."

Mr. Lambert eyed her. "That's what I mean. We wanted him to be successful."

Ella folded her hands in her lap. "But he is."

Mrs. Lambert lowered her teacup. "Perhaps we define success differently."

"Perhaps. But you should know that your son is creative and very well liked by everyone on the island. Think of parents who have children who use drugs, curse, lie and cheat—even abuse their families."

"My son doesn't have his own family," Mrs. Lambert said.

Ella drew up her shoulders. "On the island, he has a large family."

Christine watched her grandmother's dark regard brighten as her left hand shifted toward the Bible. The action lifted Christine's heart. She pictured her only weeks earlier unable to move the hand.

Ella looked at the Bible and back at the Lamberts. "And remember what the Lord says in Proverbs Sixteen. 'In his heart a man plans his course, but the Lord determines his steps.' You see, the plan isn't yours or mine to make, really. It's what the Lord has set for our purpose."

"I—I—" Will's father sputtered before stretching

his neck higher. "I don't totally agree with you, Mrs. Summers, but we each have our own philosophies."

"Oh, but this isn't a philosophy. It—"

Christine touched her grandmother's shoulder, and she ended the discussion. Christine could see it would go nowhere but cause greater stress. "Please, have some cookies. They're homemade by our neighbor."

Mrs. Lambert eyed the dish and selected one. "Thank you," she said. She examined the miniature treat and took a tiny bite.

"Dad, I'd like you to see the studio. How long are you staying?"

"Only tonight, son. We have some social engagements. You know the Christmas season."

Will gave a nod. "I sure do, Dad. So let's call a taxi and head for the store. I'd like you to see it. Then, I think, Christine is planning to cook dinner."

"Oh, no," his father said. "We planned to take you out to dinner. We saw a restaurant open on Hoban that looks acceptable. The Village Inn, I think."

Will gave Christine a discouraged look, then turned back to his parents. "We can talk about it later."

His father felt his breast pocket as if making sure no one had pickpocketed his wallet and checkbook.

Christine observed the discussion unfold as if it were a wrestling match.

His father tucked his hand inside the pocket and withdrew an envelope. "I don't want to forget this. Here's mail for you that came to the house."

"Mail?" Will reached for the envelope and checked the return address. "This is from John Skinner."

"I recognized the name," his mother said. "You graduated from high school with him."

"Right," Will said, eyeing the envelope.

Mrs. Lambert's focus settled on the letter. "I wonder what John's doing. He was such a bright boy. I know he must be involved in something worthwhile."

Will's jaw tightened as he slipped his finger under the tab and opened the envelope. He glanced at it and lay the letter on the table. "It's nothing. Just my high school class reunion announcement."

"You'll go," his mother said.

Will shook his head. "Probably not. I haven't seen those people in years."

"It's your tenth. You should go."

Tenth? His tenth high school class reunion. Christine's heart stopped, and she clamped her jaw to keep her mouth from gaping. Tenth? That meant he was— She faltered. If he graduated when he was eighteen, he was only twenty-eight. She was nearly forty.

Chapter Twelve

After Will left with his parents, Christine hurried into her bedroom and slammed the door. She'd known he had a youthful manner, but he seemed mature and capable—wonderful really. But eleven years?

She sank onto the bed and held her face in her hands. Her dreams—dreams she wanted to dispel but dreams that had persisted—sagged like the surrealistic paintings of Dali's drooping clocks. She'd be the laughing-stock of everyone if they knew she'd finally given her heart to a man nearly young enough to be her son.

And she'd kissed him on the mouth. She felt mortified.

She wanted to talk to someone. She needed someone's opinion. Ellene's face soared into her mind. She pressed the buttons on her cell. If Ellene could come for a visit, if she could meet Will and see them together, if she could— The thought hung on the air as reality flew back in her face. This was temporary. She would be leaving in another month, and Will would be a memory.

Sadness flooded her. She didn't want a memory. She wanted the impossible dream. Her thoughts wavered. Will had changed her. He'd been good for her and cared about her. Will's career could be successful in the Detroit area. Better even. Maybe... Could she influence him to even consider moving back to Detroit?

The cell address book had darkened, and she hit the buttons again and this time pushed the call symbol.

When Ellene's voice came on the line, Christine's heart picked up pace. "I need you. Can you come for a visit?"

"What's wrong?"

"Nothing. Everything." She rubbed her temple, not making sense out of anything. "I want you to meet Will, I need you to meet him. Ellene, I'm so confused. I feel so strongly about him, and we've only met. He's different, and I want to know if this is just a shipboard romance or is it real."

"It's not shipboard," Ellene said, laughter in her voice. "But you are stranded on an island and that can be dangerous. Just ask me."

"That's not funny, Ellene. Something in my heart tells me this is special." She pressed her hand against her chest, feeling thunder beneath her palm. "Ask Connor if you can come up for a couple of days. Fly up. It's not too expensive, and I'll pay your way."

"Shush. You don't have to pay my way. Let me think."

The line went silent except for Ellene's breathing, and Christine's pulse throbbing against the receiver.

"I was planning to call you," Ellene said, "but maybe it would be more fun in person. I'll check with Connor, but I don't think he'll mind at all. I'll call you."

"I'd be so grateful, Ellene. Truly. I know I sound like a babbling teenager, but it's not that. It's far from that. Today I feel very old."

"Christine, what's wrong with you? Look, I'll tell Connor it's an emergency."

"You're a dear friend," Christine said.

"You too. I'll call back with the details."

When the phone had disconnected, Christine sat staring into space, wondering how Will was faring with his family. She'd given up on making them dinner. They seemed very set on their plans, and she knew they didn't include her, and she thought it was best. She hoped Will did, too.

He needed time with his parents. Maybe once they saw his studio—his store with so many wonderful gifts—they would realize he wasn't a boy any longer.

Boy. The word zipped through her like a dart. No. He was a man. She'd spent more than two weeks with him, enjoying his company and seeing him as a peer. What was eleven years? Eleven years. She cringed at the question.

Will charged up the back steps, stomped into the hallway and slammed the door to his apartment. He took off his coat and flung it on the chair, then caved into the recliner, tilting it back and closing his eyes.

Fiasco.

He pictured the look on Christine's face when she observed his parents and him in action. Shame filled him. The Bible said to honor his parents. He hadn't, but he believed in his heart that he'd done what he had to do, and he prayed the Lord had led him in that direction. Yet it still bothered him.

One event had been a positive when—

A knock on his door drew his attention. He rose and answered it.

"Christine," he said, searching her face. "Come in."

She gave him a cautious grin and walked into the room as if she were uncomfortable.

He motioned toward a chair. "Have a seat." He leaned over and snapped on the Christmas tree lights. Anything to remind him that this was a joyous time of year. "What's up?"

She loosed a ragged sigh. "I just wondered how you fared today."

He sank into the recliner. "I'm so sorry about the dinner. I didn't think they'd be that rude, but by that time, I decided you'd be grateful not having to listen to any more of the tension."

"I understand, Will."

"They're not bad people, Christine. I know they think they have only the best in their mind for me, but their best and mine are different."

"I saw that." She lowered her head.

"My father wanted me to follow in his footsteps. That's typical of successful parents, and I tried. I went to business school for three years as I told you. Then I couldn't take it anymore. It's not what I wanted to do. I loved the arts. I knew God had given me a creative talent, but in the business administration field, it was mired by the wayside. I broke my father's heart when I told him I was dropping out of University of Michigan and going to Creative Studies. He's never accepted that decision."

"But you have a business and an art career. You've accomplished both. I would think—"

"I know. It's hard to understand. I should enjoy their visit, but it's difficult when they're so determined to force me back into their world."

"Funny thing, Will, when I first came here—" she stopped in mid-sentence as if struggling for the words. "When I first came here, I felt the same way. At least, similar to them. I questioned why anyone with a right mind would want to live on the island."

He leaned closer, wanting to make sure he'd really heard what she'd said. "Are you saying you feel differently now?"

She didn't answer but studied him for a moment, a frown settling on her face as if she were fighting the thoughts. "For you, I do. You're so suited to the island life."

"I'm glad to hear you say that. At least I know I have one person on my side."

"Two. Grandma. She adores you."

His eyes captured hers. "And you?"

"I—I admire you so much, Will. You're a wonderful…man."

She faltered, and he wondered if his parents' constant references to *boy* and *son* caused her to see him in another way. "Thanks," he said, trying to make his words sound real.

He gazed at her. Yes she was older, but not that much, he didn't think. Yet it didn't matter. He cared about her more than he could explain. Admiration wasn't what he wanted to hear. Yes, her admiration was nice, and so was respect, but he wanted to be loved.

Christine broke the silence. "Was the whole time with them as stressed as it was here?"

"You mean my parents?"

"Yes. After you left, did it—"

"Get better? Yes. In fact, I was just sitting here thinking about it. When I showed them the store and my studio, both of them seemed to be knocked sideways. I don't know what they thought I had here, but they were impressed. I could see my mother's mental calculator adding the value of the large windows hanging in the store."

Christine chuckled, and it sounded so good to him.

"My dad began grilling me about sales. I showed him my books. His eyes widened like an owl. I think the part that bothered him was the quiet winter. He began talking marketing. That part's just not in me."

"I know," she said.

Will realized it was in her, and she'd mentioned wanting to talk with him about ideas. He hoped not tonight. He couldn't bear to hear any more criticism right now. "How was your day?"

"Good. My friend Ellene is coming next Friday for the weekend. I think you'll like her."

"I'm glad she's coming," he said, not meaning it. He'd have to share her with someone for the weekend, and he wanted to keep her for himself.

"Are your parents leaving in the morning?" she asked.

"I thought about meeting them for brunch. They mentioned eating before they catch the early-afternoon ferry. They don't go to church."

"I wondered about that."

"They attend church occasionally, but they don't have the same kind of relationship with God that I have."

"I guessed that from the conversation with Grandma." She looked uneasy. "I'm afraid they don't like me very much. Still, I'm sorry I didn't have a chance to say goodbye."

"Then join us. I think my dad admired you. He's hard to read, but remember, he thought you had brains—which is what I seem to lack."

She grinned.

"Church service is early," he said. "I'm not going to meet them until eleven. Please come with me."

"I'll talk with Grandma. Maybe I will if you're sure they won't mind."

He didn't really care if they did.

She rose and moved toward the door. "You need to rest. It's been a difficult day, I know."

Will stood and caught her hand, pulling her closer. She seemed to resist, then in the next moment relaxed in his arms. He didn't want to push his luck. Will lowered his lips and kissed her temple. He sensed he should take it easy or risk driving her away. Had it been his parents' behavior or something else that had created a new wedge between them?

"Are you sure they won't be upset?" Christine climbed off Will's sled and joined him as he headed into Sinclair's.

"I think they'll be fine," he said, opening the door.

The sweep of heat washed over her as they entered.

"There they are," Will said, pointing toward a table on the far side of the room.

His father noticed him and motioned to his wife. She looked up, a mixture of surprise and question on her face.

"We didn't know if you were coming," his father said, gesturing to the two extra chairs.

"I wasn't sure if I would, but Christine wanted to say goodbye and so do I."

"That's thoughtful," his mother said.

Christine tried to read a tone in her voice, but she didn't hear one.

Mrs. Lambert turned to her. "I was rather impressed with Will's business."

The statement surprised Christine and opened the door for Christine's thoughts. "Amazing, really. Will's work is exquisite. He can price his work at a high rate because of the quality, and he's innovative. Besides the stained-glass pieces, he's created other art—jewelry and decorative plates and bowls—by fusing glass. I hope he showed them to you."

She realized her mouth raced like a revving engine, and she caught her breath to let them respond.

Mrs. Lambert glanced at her husband, then Will. "Yes, I believe he did show us."

"I brought out a few pieces," Will said. "Mother particularly liked the fluted bowl in the shades of coral and pink. I think you saw that, didn't you?"

Christine nodded. "Yes. It's lovely. All of your work is."

"You're prejudiced." He gave her a private look.

The waitress arrived with coffee and halted their conversation while she told them about the Sunday buffet. When she walked away, the conversation continued as if it had never stopped.

"I worry about the winter months. No income really." His father pushed his coffee cup with his finger. "A man needs year-round work."

"Dad, I told you I have a number of projects to complete for the holidays. People call me for custom orders, and when I'm not busy with those, I need the time to work on new stock for the summer. I do a tremendous business then."

"Yes, I saw that," he said, pulling his finger from

the cup and leaning back in the chair as if calculating what he wanted to say next.

"Let's check out the buffet," Will suggested, standing and pulling out Christine's chair as she rose.

His mother and father followed, and they went through the line selecting their breakfast fare. Will looked relieved that the earlier conversation had ended.

At the table, they spent quiet moments delving into the good food, with comments made about the various dishes and little else. When Will's father pushed his plate back, he studied Christine. "Do you enjoy island life, Christine?"

The question surprised her, and she choked on her drink. "I think the island life is wonderful for some people." She set her fork on the edge of her plate. "But I have mixed feelings for me, personally. My work is in Southfield."

She looked at Will and weighed the question. "For Will this is a perfect setting. He has the winter's quiet to prepare for the mass of tourists that arrive in May and stay until October. He loves it here. I can't imagine him in another setting." The words pained her, but she knew they were true. "Some of us can live in the city and thrive on the big corporations. Some prefer the small towns and can thrive as well. I wish—" What? She wished so many things.

Mr. Lambert eyed her. "You wish you had the stomach for island life?" The gaze drifted from her to Will, and she sensed he noticed the heated flush rising up her neck.

"I wish I didn't have to cope with the stress of big-city life and still have the benefits."

Mr. Lambert shook his head. "You're an honest woman."

"Will," his mother said, drawing his attention, "I will admit that I'm impressed with your talent. I had envisioned your work so differently."

Christine's heart jumped, hearing his mother's confession. She tried to listen to the private conversation, but his father caught her eye and leaned toward her in a conspiratorial manner. "We know Will has talent," he said, speaking in a near whisper, "but we'd like him to stretch his wings in a more aggressive business style. Think of what he could do."

She felt her face pull into a frown. She'd tried to suggest those things. "But that's not what Will—"

"Wants," his father said, completing her statement. "I know, but you're a wise woman. My wife senses you have feelings for Will, and his life here and yours there—"

"I respect Will's talent, and he's a wonderful friend, but we barely know each other."

"You're a woman with some sense in her head. We think you could influence him to—"

Christine patted his arm to stop him. "I said I respect Will. That means I also respect his decision. I have no idea where our relationship could lead, but I know one thing for sure. If I really loved him, I would never drag him away from something this important to him. Then my love wouldn't be true."

His father's eyes darkened. "This is more of your Bible talk, I suppose."

Christine couldn't help but smile. "Bible talk? That's my grandmother. I came here like you, Mr. Lambert, a weak Christian."

He drew back, his brows lifting.

"I'm sorry for being honest." She glanced to make sure Will's attention was on his mother. It was, and she returned to her private dialogue. "Yes, it's in the Bible, but I mean what I say. I rarely went to church. I was a title Christian."

His frown deepened.

Christine didn't let that stop her. "Will has a deep faith, as does my grandmother, and recently I heard her description of love, and I went to the Word and studied it for myself because I needed to know the truth. Love is not self-seeking. It keeps no record of wrongs. Love protects and hopes and trusts." She looked at Will's father. "I trust Will. I trust that he knows what he's doing. If you love him, you will too."

He leaned back, his gaze connected with hers, but she saw a new look in his eyes. He didn't speak, and Christine feared she'd done greater harm than good.

Finally, he leaned forward. "You've made a point."

"Thank you," she said, releasing a pent-up breath as the waitress arrived with their bill.

Chapter Thirteen

"I'm grateful for those church ladies," Will said, standing beside Christine in his studio.

She chuckled, knowing what he meant, because she agreed.

"I noticed they're even helping with her therapy now. Those women deserve stars in their crowns."

"I told them that, but they love it. Grandma is a blessed woman to have so many people care about her."

"The only thing I don't like." he said, pulling supplies from drawers beneath his workbench, "is the quicker she gets better, the faster you'll be leaving."

Christine didn't want to think of the inevitable either. Her mind shot back to the conversation with Will's father five days earlier. Will had never asked what they were talking about, and, being preoccupied with his mother's conversation, she hoped he hadn't noticed.

She shook her head. "Don't think about that now.

I'm here until my vacation's over, and then longer if I use a family medical leave, and I'm thinking I may do that. All I can hope is Chet doesn't push too hard. He could make life very difficult for me at the office if he follows through."

"I don't want to see that happen, Christine. I know you love your work."

She looked at the sincerity in his eyes, and her pulse skipped. She'd always said she loved her work, but watching Will in the studio—the joy he had in creating, the lack of stress, the delight in living— sometimes she wondered about her situation at Creative Productions. Still, that's the work she knew, and that's where she excelled.

"Okay, ready to learn about making beads?" He slipped on his safety glasses and lit a torch he'd clamped to his worktable.

Beads. She'd wanted time to talk with him. She'd thought about what she'd said to his father, and she told herself she wasn't trying to change him, but just make things better for him. But she observed his eagerness with the beads. "Sure," she said, though her heart wasn't in it.

"I've already coated the mandrel with bead release. That's a fireproof coating."

"Great, but what's a mandrel?"

His mouth curved to a grin. "This metal rod." He lifted it from the equipment on the table. "You need this to make beads."

"Okay," she said, feeling the heat of the torch.

She watched him heat the mandrel, then warm the glass rods, rotating them until they formed what appeared to be a honey-type liquid blob. As the glass melted, he touched the mandrel tip to the glass and rotated it to form a circle. When it reached what he apparently thought was the right size, he pulled away the rod and continued to rotate the bead to a smooth surface. She felt her mouth gape at the ease with which he created the lovely bauble.

"Want to try this?"

She stepped back. "I don't think so, Will. That's your talent. Mine is advertising and marketing. Now that, I could help you with."

He moved back the mandrel and rolled the bead on a special surface, then lowered it onto a cooling mixture. When he looked at her, disappointment had registered on his face. "Did my father succeed in influencing you?"

She drew back at his question. "No. Not at all. I told you a long time ago I had some ideas. I would never do that to you." Her shoulders tensed with his accusation.

In a heartbeat, he lowered the mandrel and turned off the torch, then drew her to him. "I'm sorry, Christine. I shouldn't have said that."

She felt as if he'd slapped her.

"I have no excuse," he said, his voice strained. "I saw my father talking to you at the restaurant. He seemed intense, and so were you. You haven't mentioned the conversation, and I hated to ask. I figured you'd say something."

"I'm sorry I didn't." She hadn't wanted to tell him that his father had tried to influence her. She'd prayed for reconciliation between them.

"When you didn't say anything, I started assuming what he talked about. Naturally I figured he wanted you to coerce me back to Detroit."

Her muscles knotted as disappointment spread over her. "I'm sorry you'd think I'd do that, Will."

"No, Christine. It's me. I get this way with my dad. My mother had eased a little, and I thought maybe—"

"I defended you. I told your father that real love had nothing to do with forcing someone's will. It had to do with trust and confidence in them. I'd never try to manipulate you, and I'm disappointed that you think I would do that."

He stepped away and turned his back. "I was wrong to accuse you, but you know, I've sensed you pulling away since my parents came. I realized our friendship is…temporary. It's—"

"I don't want to hear that. Please. I treasure the time we've spent together. I've changed, and I attribute that to my grandmother and you. I've learned something about myself. It's nothing to do with how I feel about you. It's—" She stopped herself. Not now. She needed to think, to weigh her feelings and take a long look at her life. She needed time.

"Let's leave it at that." He picked the bead from the fiber and rolled it between his fingers, then dropped it into her hand. "So what are your thoughts?"

"About us?"

"No. You mentioned your ideas."

Her ideas seemed so unimportant now. She weighed the value of causing more tension between them with sharing the strategies she'd thought of earlier. She couldn't help herself. Marketing was her work.

"This has no reflection on your father's opinion. When I first came here and saw the great merchandise you have—all those wonderful pieces of art—I thought about marketing. I know you have a captive audience in the summer, but you could enhance the late autumn, winter and early spring months by using the Internet."

"You mean selling online?"

She nodded, her enthusiasm growing. "All you need is a Web site that offers photographs of your work— the jewelry, sun catchers, small windows, vases, things easy to mail—and a brief description with the price. Once you know the shipping cost, you can set up a secure site and use charge cards or an Internet bank service, and that's it. You could hire someone to do packaging and handling or do it yourself."

Her heart pumped at the thought of how his sales could rise. "Do you know how many people shop on the Internet? It's amazing."

His eyes widened and glazed. "I don't mean to sound ignorant, but Christine, I don't know anything about creating Web sites and finding secure sites. I'm an artist."

"But some people do." She swallowed, fearing where she was headed. "I do. I could help you get started. You're a great photographer. You can take the photos, or I can, and I'll—"

"Christine, I'm not sure I want to do this. Once you're gone, then what do I do?"

"I—" She stopped herself, seeing the expression on his face. She remembered what Ellene had said. "You have a wonderful business, Will. I don't know why I'm even suggesting this. It's just a gold mine for you." His expression reminded her of the truth. Will didn't seem to want a gold mine. He loved his simple life, so why change it?

"It's not that I don't appreciate your ideas," he said, relaxing and moving closer. He took her in his arms and kissed the top of her head. "You're suggesting what is so natural for you. I need to think about the reason I would do this. Why complicate my life?"

She wondered if she had already complicated his life by just being there. Christine lifted her gaze to his and her stomach rolled with a sweet sensation. "You're right, Will."

"As always," he said, a smile brightening his face. "Let me think. I need some time to weigh what you've said."

I need some time. So did she. Christine shrugged, wishing she could learn to keep her ideas to herself.

"Don't be sad," he said, tilting her chin upward. His gaze drifted to her lips, and her heart squeezed in anticipation.

Will's mouth bent to hers, but this time the gentle

touch deepened. He held her close, his hand cupping her head, his fingers plying her hair while his free hand held her shoulders with a tenderness that made her knees weak. Emotion took away her breath, and her lungs cried for air.

Will eased back and kissed the tip of her nose. "I'm thinking," he said, his mouth so close she could feel his lips move against hers.

A smile tugged at the corner of her mouth, but before it could reach the surface, his lips met hers again.

Dear Lord, she thought, *I'm lost in this man's arms. I've never felt this way, but how can it ever be? He's so young. I'm so much older. My heart is fighting my head, and I'm so afraid I'll be hurt again. Help me, Lord.*

"Should we leave for the airport?" Will asked.

"Ellene said she wouldn't take off until noon, so we have time…"

Christine looked gorgeous with her legs tucked beneath her in his recliner. Will wished he owned a sofa so he could hold her in his arms. Maybe his parents were right about one thing at least. He needed a bigger apartment if he was ever going to find someone to share his life.

He patted his lap. "Come here a second."

"Why?"

"I want you near me."

"That's silly. We'll break the chair."

"Not so, but if we do, I'll buy another one."

She laughed, her long hair sweeping over her face as she gave him a coy look as if playing hard to get.

"Please," he said, sending her a coaxing smile.

She pulled herself from the recliner and sauntered toward him, an elfish look in her eye. "This is silly, you know."

"Sometimes it's fun to be silly." He reached forward and grasped her hand, pulling her down.

Christine rested her head on his shoulder, and he wrapped his arms around her, loving the feeling of being close to her.

"See. This is perfect."

She wriggled as if to get comfortable. "I'm sorry about the bead making, Will. Maybe one day I can concentrate. I'd love to learn how to make them."

"Like you said, it's not your expertise."

"No, but I expected you to build a Web site and sell online. That's not yours, either. I have a controlling nature, and I'm not really happy with it anymore."

"I'm happy with everything about you."

"That's because you're so…you. It's your natural way. You have every fruit of the spirit. I wish I knew how you do it."

"I don't do it, Christine," he said, running his finger along the arm of her sweater. "It's the Lord."

"But how do you get Him to do it?"

He couldn't help but laugh at her question. "I don't know. I study the Word. I pray for God's direction."

"I've been doing that. I really have."

"And I allow the Lord to work in me. Your grandmother talks so often about the fruits of the spirit, and they're almost inseparable from Jesus's new commandment."

"You mean there's an eleventh commandment?" She tilted her head upward, smiling at him.

He shook his head. "You're teasing," he said, enjoying the sweet scent of her perfume. "Jesus said 'I give you a new commandment and that is to love one another as I have loved you.' So it's easy. We respond to things in the best manner we can to emulate Jesus."

"Easy? I find that very hard."

"No one's perfect, but we can try."

She swung her legs downward and shifted to sit more upright. "Do you mean that by trying to be more like Jesus we become closer to Him?"

"I think so. I know that the Lord is beside me now." He brushed his fingers against her soft cheek.

"If you have all of us on your lap, this chair is really going to break."

He gave her a teasing poke. "Stop. We're being serious now. Jesus is always with me. It's that personal kind of relationship that people talk about. I can just toss out my concerns, and I know He is here and He hears me. He's beside you, too."

She lowered her head. "Funny, but since I've been on the island, I can better understand what you're saying. Maybe it's less distractions or—"

"Less competitiveness, less media, less traffic, less of the things that aren't important. On an island, you depend on people—on personal relationships. That's what's important. Then kindness and compassion are natural."

"Why are you so young yet so wise?"

Will felt her tense as if the comment was something she hadn't wanted to deal with. Her reaction rocked him. Was that why she'd become so withdrawn after brunch with his father? He'd felt it, then watched it fade as they spent time together. But it really hadn't faded at all.

"Do you want to talk about this?" he asked.

She lowered her head, dismay on her face. "I'm sorry I said anything. I've been trying to let it not bother me. We're only friends. We can—"

"Christine."

She faltered when he said her name, and she lifted her gaze to his, her eyes filled with concern.

"Do you really believe we're only friends?" He waited, watching her face shift from one emotion to another, until he saw tears well in her eyes.

"Please," Will said, drawing her against his chest again, "don't be upset. Age is a state of mind. I guessed a while ago I was little younger than you, but I hoped it wouldn't bother you."

"When your parents were here and I heard some of the conversation, I calculated you're twenty-eight or so." She looked at him with question.

"I'll be twenty-nine in January."

"Do you know how old I am?"

"I don't care."

"Yes, you do."

"You mean too much to me to let something as finite as age affect our relationship. What we have is precious."

"What do we have, Will? That's what I want to know. I live in metro Detroit. You're up here. I can never see you leaving the island. I can't picture me living here. I'm bossy and stressed much of the time. You're easygoing and so wonderful."

"Remember what I said. Let the Lord handle this. I don't have all the answers, but if the feelings I have for you are real, then I know God has the answer. I trust in Him."

He felt her tense against him. She turned and clasped his face in her hands. "I can't believe I'm saying this, but I trust Him, too."

He drew his fingers along her hair and brushed the softness of her neck. "I can't tell you how happy I am to hear you say that."

They were silent a moment, each perhaps in their own thoughts.

Then she stirred. "I'm thirty-nine, Will. I could almost be your mother."

Chapter Fourteen

Christine looked at Will's startled expression, and it broke her heart. He could deny it all he wanted, but she could tell he hadn't realized exactly how old she was.

"You're being dramatic," he said. "A few years means nothing to me."

She slipped from his lap and headed toward the kitchenette for water. "I'm just making a point."

"I know, and I'm ignoring it. I don't care if you're fifty. I care about you, and that's all that matters."

With a glass in her hand, she turned and studied him, wondering if the expression she'd seen had been only her imagination. "You were shocked when I told you my age. Admit it."

"What shocked me was the thought of your being my mother. I would have been very disappointed."

"Disappointed? Why?"

"Because then I would never have known you as I do."

Christine swung back to the faucet and ran the tap as she weighed his words, facing his determination but pondering the wisdom.

She took a long drink, then glanced at her watch. "We'd better get to the airport. Ellene will be waiting."

Will rose and grabbed his jacket from the back of a kitchen chair. "I'd like you to think about what I've said, Christine. This conversation isn't over."

She shook her head. "Will, let's just drop it. I have so much going in my life that I don't know which end is up. I like you. You know that."

He reached for her arm and stared into her eyes, his question obvious.

"Okay, so it's more than like. I really care about you, and I wish things were different, but they're not. I can't answer the questions I know you have. I want to enjoy what we have. Can we do that?"

Will was silent as he zipped his jacket.

"Please," she said.

"For now. Enjoy your friend's visit for the weekend, but we can't stop, Christine. My heart's on the line, and—"

Christine pressed her finger against his lips. "Mine is, too, Will."

His gaze captured hers, and she felt drawn like a hummingbird to nectar. She leaned closer and brushed a kiss on his lips.

They stood a moment without speaking, then he pressed his palm to her cheek. "We'd better go. Dress warm."

She slipped into her boots and jacket, wrapped the red scarf around her neck and covered her ears with a new pair of red earmuffs.

As they strode outside, she pulled her gloves from her pocket. They'd agreed to her driving her grandmother's snowmobile so Ellene could ride with Will. She'd warned Ellene to dress warm, and she hoped her friend knew what that meant.

The sun's warmth hadn't penetrated the nippy breeze, and Christine shivered, but once settled on the sled, the heat of excitement embraced her as she started the engine and waited for it to warm. Will gave a wave, and she followed him, opening the throttle and gliding to the street, then zooming toward the airport.

Will headed left to Hoban Road, slowed near Annex and made another left. She could see the airport driveway to her right, and her excitement grew as she anticipated seeing Ellene. She needed a friend. She needed an honest appraisal of the crazy thoughts leading her into an unknown way of life. She needed common sense, and she'd find that in her friend.

When they pulled up to the terminal building, she turned off the engine and hurried up the walk. Will trailed behind her, giving her a chance to greet Ellene alone, she guessed.

Ellene appeared at the doorway, her wild dark hair held bound by a knitted cap. "I'm ready," she said, opening her arms to Christine, who ran into them with the speed of light.

"Thanks for coming." Christine looked at her and noticed her attention had shifted beyond her shoulder. Christine turned around to see Will's smiling face.

"Ellene, this is Will Lambert. Will, Ellene Farraday."

They moved closer and shook hands, each eyeing the other.

"Will's going to be your taxi."

"Really," she said. "That sounds interesting."

"My sled will be," he said, understanding her humor. "Do you have luggage?"

"Just this case." She extended her carry-on bag. "I'm only here for a weekend."

Will chuckled. "Christine said she was only here for a week and look what happened."

"My husband would never forgive me," she said with a smile.

"Ready to face the elements?"

"As ready as I'll ever be," Ellene said, linking arms with Christine as they headed toward the sleds.

An icy shiver charged down Christine's back, and she feared it wasn't the wind but the outcome of Ellene's visit. What did she expect from her friend? She wanted Ellene to like Will, and yet she feared she would. The paradox made no sense, but the worry felt real.

Now that she'd asked for help, perhaps she'd sought the wrong person. She thought of what Will had said earlier. Jesus walked beside him every minute. Why couldn't she let the Lord handle her confusion and not drag Ellene into the quandary?

* * *

"I've never liked Scrabble," Will said as Christine added up her twenty-three-letter word. "She makes everyone else look like they're ignorant."

She couldn't help but grin at his upset. "No I don't. I have a strategic eye."

Ella concentrated on the game, gathered her letters together and placed her word on the board.

"You can't use 'saith,'" Christine said. "The rules say no foreign words." She knew the word but loved teasing her grandmother.

Everyone laughed. "It's in the Bible, Christine," Ella said. "And God's Word can't be wrong."

"She got you," Will said, studying his letters for his turn. "It's getting late." He looked around the table and ended with Christine. "Is this about over?"

"You want to give up and let me win?" Christine wrinkled her nose at him.

"Sounds good to me. You're going to win anyway."

"For someone who's known you only a few weeks," Ellene said, "this man has your number."

Will chuckled and banged the table. The board loped upward as words divided and skidded across its face.

"I suppose we have to quit now." Christine shook her head. "You did that on purpose."

"I really didn't, but I think it was providence."

They slid their letters into the box, and Christine folded the board while Ellene gathered the letter stands, putting everything inside the game box.

Will stood. "Now, I think it's time for me to say

good-night." He leaned over and grasped Ellene's hand. "It's nice to get to know one of Christine's friends. Your husband sounds like a man I'd like to meet."

"Maybe you will," she said, giving a telling glance toward Christine, then back to him.

Christine cringed with her obvious meaning. They hadn't talked yet. She'd avoided saying anything to Ellene, because she wanted her to get to know Will without her influence.

Will tipped his imaginary hat and slipped into the foyer.

Christine heard the back door close, and she looked at Ellene, wanting so badly to talk but not with her grandmother present.

When she turned toward her grandmother, Ella gave a wide yawn. "I think I'll get cozy in bed and read my Bible for a while before I go to sleep. You girls need time to talk."

"Don't rush off because of me," Ellene said.

"No, dear, not at all. Shuffling around with one leg still not cooperating is very tiring. And you saw the workout Christine gave me with my therapy."

"She is a taskmaster," Ellene said.

"Anyway," she continued, "I love to read God's Word all snuggled up in bed."

"Let me help, Grandma," Christine said, rising and handing her the footed cane they'd moved out of the way.

She took her grandmother's arm to steady her and

they made their way to the door. "I'll be right back," Christine said over her shoulder.

Christine's heart had lifted as she watched her grandmother's improvement. Her left hand had more strength, and though her fingers needed still greater coordination, she had some use of them.

When her grandmother had undressed, Christine hung up her clothing or dropped items in the hamper, then helped her with the buttons on her flannel gown. Christine shifted her grandmother's Bible closer on her nightstand, then leaned down to give her a kiss on the cheek. "Good night, Grandma."

"Good night, Christine. I hope you and Ellene have a good talk. I think she likes Will."

Christine bit her cheek. She should be happy, but her emotions headed off to dark corners. "I think she does, too."

"But I want you to remember one thing." Her grandmother lifted the Bible with her right hand and rested it on the blanket. "Proverbs says, 'There is no wisdom, no insight, no plan that can succeed against the Lord.'"

Christine stood a moment, trying to decipher what her grandmother meant.

"You don't understand?"

"I—"

"I know you invited Ellene here because you're concerned about Will."

Christine thought a moment. "No, not Will. I'm concerned about me."

"It's one and the same, dear. You see Will in your

future, and it frightens you. You want your friend's advice. Just remember that all the advice in the world cannot shake the Lord's path for you."

"I know, Grandma, it's just—" She paused, trying to decide if she wanted to say it or not. "Do you realize how old Will is? Do you know how old I am?"

Her grandmother chuckled. "I've never seen anything in the Bible that states who has to be older or younger, but remember what I've told you before—a person plans his course, but the Lord determines his steps."

Christine drew back. How many times had she been reminded that she could plan until she turned purple but the Lord guided her steps.

"Will may be younger than you, Christine, but he is a God-fearing Christian man who thinks the world of you. I've seen it. What is more important, that a man be older than a woman or that a man treats the woman as if she is a gift from heaven?"

A ragged breath shivered from Christine. She touched her grandmother's hand. "Thanks, Grandma. I'll heed your words."

"That's all we want, dear."

"We?"

"The Lord and me."

A faint grin found Christine as she placed the table lamp remote button closer to her grandmother. "I love you," she whispered as she closed the door and headed down the hallway, realizing she couldn't sneak anything past her grandmother.

"That didn't take too long," Christine said, walking into the living room.

Ellene had turned on the television but snapped it off and laid the remote onto the lamp table. "Tell me. I'm curious."

Christine faltered. "Curious? About what?"

"What's your problem?"

"You mean with Will?"

"Yes. You told me you were so different. I understand he lives here and you live in Royal Oak. That's different, but personality-wise, the two of you fit like gloves. I love his humor, and you play off it like a fine-tuned instrument." She paused and leaned forward, sincerity filling her face. "Christine, the man's a gem."

Christine fell back against the sofa cushion. "I know. I know."

Ellene rose and shifted to her side. "So what is it? The island versus the big city?"

"Yes, part of it. That is a problem. My work. His work. He doesn't want to leave the island. I can't work here."

Ellene took her hands. "How important is that, Christine? Does your career mean everything in the world to you?"

"Certainly it does." She lowered her head. "It always has until—"

"Until what?"

Christine struggled with her thoughts. What was the real problem? She knew Will had strong feelings for her, but could she trust him? She wanted to say yes, but she feared being wrong. She'd been wrong before. And then the age issue. Ellene hadn't mentioned their ages.

Ellene waited, then asked again.

"Part of it is reality. You remember what happened with Chet. Do I keep my head when my heart's involved?"

"But Will isn't Chet. He's as far from being Chet as I am from being the Queen of England."

"I know. He's a wonderful Christian. I'm working on being a better one myself." A deep sigh escaped her. "It's my career, too. Who would I be without it?"

"A wife who supports her husband's work. A mother someday."

"A mother?" The age factor shook her again. "I'm nearly forty. That's another issue."

"If you are in love and you marry, you still have time. I know the clock is ticking, but lots of women make the decision later in life."

"This is stupid," Christine said, realizing how far astray the conversation had gone. "He hasn't asked me to marry him."

"Not yet, but I can see it coming."

The comment smacked her between the eyes. "You mean you really see that?"

"I'd be blind if I didn't."

The news made her reel. She knew Will cared. She cared, but— "Okay, but do you see nothing else about age? You don't see any problems?"

Ellene frowned. "Are we playing guessing games?" She shook her head. "Is he younger than you?"

Christine veered back. "You have to ask?"

"Yes, I guess I do. Both of you have a youthful spirit—especially here, Christine. I've never seen you so lighthearted. When I saw you on the snowmobile, laughing and later playing Scrabble— You two are like kids."

"That's because he is a kid."

Ellene froze, then recovered. "He might be younger, but he's a man. Either that, or I'm deluded."

"He's twenty-eight. Twenty-nine in January. I'm eleven years older than he is."

"Ten after his birthday," she said, a light tone in her voice. She wrapped her arms around Christine's shoulders. "My dear friend, don't hold back a chance at pure happiness because of a few years, an island life, and a career. I want to tell you my life is tremendous since I fell in love again with Connor."

"You do look wonderful," Christine said, noticing the bloom in her cheeks. "You look as if life has been good."

"It's been more than that, and I'll tell you in a minute, but let's finish this. So the man is younger. If it's not important to him, then it shouldn't be to you. If he's as strong a Christian as you say, he won't play lightly with marriage. Christians believe their vows—until death parts them. I can't envision him playing games with marriage."

Christine knotted her hands and dropped them to her lap. "But does he know his mind?"

Ellene lowered her arms and drew back. "Here's the truth. I think Will is a catch. I think he could make a wonderful husband and a great father. I think he's as honest as he is sincere, but I have doubts."

"You do?" Christine felt her heart tug. She wanted to know those doubts, but she wanted Will more. Her mind tossed like a tree in a hurricane.

"If you're this unsure, then I think you should be cautious. You want a career and the big city. You can't have that here. You can manipulate him to move—then you can have both—but should you? I think not. If the love isn't strong enough to stand the test, then it won't hold up under marriage."

Christine rose and paced the floor. She'd said the same to Will's father. She didn't know what she wanted anymore. Fear charged through her thoughts and nailed her to the floor. "You said your marriage was wonderful. You were happy. So why the change of heart?"

"I am happy. I'm ecstatic. Marriage is wonderful and blessed, but it's not perfect and it's not easy."

"There isn't much that is." Christine pressed her fingertips against her temple to quell the pounding.

"No, but all of the problems are minor to the joy. That's why love can see you through it all, but the love must be sure and strong."

Christine's mind glided back to her talks with Will, the sled rides, watching him work in the studio, seeing his tenderness with her grandmother, his loving kisses. How could she push that away because of fear? "I need to think, Ellene. I thought it was the age that bothered me, and it does. But you're right— what's age? My grandmother reminded me—more than once—that I can plan my life down to the nth degree, but it's God in charge."

"Your grandmother's right."

Christine returned and sank to the sofa. She pushed the palms of her hands into her eyes, willing the headache to vanish. While she thought, Ellene remained quiet like the good friend that she was.

"Thanks," Christine said finally. "Those were things I needed to hear, and it will give me food for thought."

"I'm glad."

Ellene's smile radiated, and Christine looked at her sitting beside her like a woman who had a secret bursting to be released. Her mind shot back to Ellene's earlier comment. "When I said you looked as if life has been good, you said it's been more than that. So what does that mean?"

"Can't you guess?"

Christine eyed her again as the truth fell into her mind. "Really?" She glanced at her belly and noticed the faint roundness. "You're pregnant."

"I am. We're so excited and so is Caitlin."

Christine threw her arms around Ellene's neck. "Do you know what the baby is?"

"No, but I'd love a boy for Connor. Still I adore Caitlin as if she were my own and would be thrilled with a little girl. Whatever the Lord blesses us with is fine with me."

"I'm so happy for you. A baby. It's wonderful."

"You can't believe how wonderful. My career has taken a back step now. I don't care about proving anything like I did a year ago. I wanted my dad to be proud of me—a woman contractor. Dad is, I know, but he's even more thrilled to be a grandfather."

"Our values change, I guess."

"That's what I've been telling you, my friend. Weigh what's important in your life. Love and family. Career and success. Sometimes a little of both, but God's will be done."

"I'll say amen to that." Christine closed her eyes and gave Ellene another hug. Warmth spread through her, knowing God had the solution, and she needed a clear answer from the Lord.

Chapter Fifteen

Will stood back near the sled, letting Christine say her goodbye.

"I can't tell you how much I appreciate your coming, Ellene." Christine hugged her friend, then gave her belly a tender pat. "I can't wait to meet the new little Farraday. Keep me posted."

"Godmother?" Ellene asked, giving Christine a questioning look.

"I'd be honored. Give Caitlin a hug, and tell Connor how happy I am."

"I will," she said, stepping backward toward Will.

Will helped Ellene into the sled with less assurance than he had when she arrived. Then he hadn't realized she carried a child in her belly, and he worried about the bumpy ride. "You sure you'll be okay?"

She grinned up at him from the sled. "I arrived two days ago. I haven't changed that much." She gave another wave to Christine. "See you when you get back."

Christine moved forward. "Are you sure you don't mind my not riding to the airport? If I hadn't checked my e-mail this morning, I wouldn't know about the snafu at my office."

"No problem. I'll be boarding as soon as I arrive. Love you."

"Love you back." Christine waved.

Will revved the engine, rolling forward a minute before making sure Ellene was settled and comfortable.

"I'm ready," she said. "Anytime."

Will sent a wave to Christine and glided toward the end of the driveway, then headed onto the road.

The day was the warmest it had been since Ellene had arrived. They'd spent Saturday at Will's studio while Ellene raved about his work and agreed with Christine about the Internet sales. He'd given it thought but still hadn't felt comfortable with the idea. As a businessman, he knew expanding sales had value, but his inexperience with the Internet set him back.

Ellene clung to him tightly, the way Christine had when she first started riding. Now Christine's hold had lessened, not from foolishness but with confidence. He loved the feel of Christine behind him on the sled.

Trying to talk seemed pointless, but he checked on Ellene once in a while to make sure she felt secure, and in minutes, they'd arrived at the airport.

He helped her from the sled while his mind clung

to Christine and her need to call the office. He wondered if they were putting pressure on her to return, and he feared what she would do.

"I enjoyed meeting you so much, Will," Ellene said as he carried her bag to the terminal.

"Same here." But he wanted to know so much more. He opened the door, and they stepped inside the terminal.

Ellene turned to face him. "Be patient with Christine. She's finding her way."

He knew he'd frowned at her comment, because the expression on her face changed. "I'm not sure what you mean?"

Ellene smiled. "You think a lot of her, I've deducted."

"Yes. Very much."

"She cares very much about you, but she's dealing with some old fears and some new ones." She shook her head and chuckled. "I know I sound cryptic, but trust me. She's looking to the Lord for answers, and that can't be bad."

Will smiled back. "That's good news. We all have problems. I have my own problems." He saw the question on her face. "I've been open with Christine. There are no surprises."

"Good," she said, glancing out the window at the runway. "I suppose I'd better get going."

Ellene extended her hand, and Will grasped it,

feeling a sense of peace. "Thanks for your candid comments."

Ellene held her finger to her lips. "Those were between you and me, okay?"

He nodded and handed her the carry-on bag. "Safe flight," he called as she headed to the tarmac.

She wiggled her fingers in a wave and exited through the doorway.

Will watched her go, hoping she was right. What had she and Christine talked about and what had been said? He knew the problem had been careers and the island. Now they'd added the age factor.

Age? He couldn't see that as a factor. Christine was spring to him. She was blossoming flowers and humming bees, the wings of birds and the flutter of butterfly wings. She was a delight, even those first days when her attitude nearly darkened the glow of the real woman.

Will turned and headed back to the sled. New snowflakes twirled on the wind, and he tugged on his gloves while feeling a smile grow on his face. He'd become almost poetic thinking of Christine. With her, his creativity flew. He could only imagine what it might be like to have her in his life always.

Christine clutched the telephone against her ear. "Tell me the truth, Sandy. What's happening?"

She listened to Sandy's dire story of Chet's tactics.

"He wants to replace me on the project or for good?" Christine asked. "He can't do that."

Sandy's voice lowered. "I shouldn't be telling you this, but you've been a good friend. Chet is really on a rampage. I can't make sense out of it."

Christine's mind swam with possibilities. "Do you think his job is on the line? We've done well with the clients, haven't we? I thought my last meeting on the Dorset project went well. They gave us the contract."

"I know. I don't have a clue."

"If he's in trouble, then I know he'll try to blame us. Watch out for yourself, Sandy. Chet comes across like cream, but underneath, he's cottage cheese."

Sandy chuckled. "You don't like cottage cheese, do you?"

"I hate it, but it's an analogy. He's not as smooth as he tries to make himself out to be."

"I got it," Sandy said.

"Just watch it, and keep me posted if you learn anything."

"I will," she said, but Christine heard a tone in her voice.

"I know I'm going to take off more time. I talked to my mom this morning. She's making progress, but she can't be any help to my grandmother while she's taking care of her own problems."

"I'm sorry you're going through all of this."

"Thanks. I'm okay with it."

"That's good. I'm beginning to think you're right,

Christine." She lowered her voice again. "Chet's gone to a corporate meeting in Chicago. I wonder if they've caught up with him. Did you know they're requiring the execs to turn in a monthly strategic-planning report on their teams? That's not just what we're doing but what he's doing."

"You're kidding."

"No, we've been hearing the buzz for a couple of weeks."

Christine massaged the back of her neck. "I doubt if Chet can cover himself with corporate." She paused, her heart sinking. "Unless he can prove he has a few incompetents under him."

"But you've already answered that. We've had good campaigns. They're not stupid at corporate."

She weighed what Sandy had said. "Chet's going to have to cover himself some other way."

"So we all need to keep our eyes open. I'm glad you called, Christine."

"When does Chet get back into the office?"

"Wednesday afternoon, he said."

"I'll call him then. We both know he's up to some-thing. I can't believe I fell for that man."

Silence hung over the line.

Christine's arms tingled. "Sandy?"

"You weren't the only one." Sandy's lengthy sigh rattled over the phone.

"No. Not you." Sadness flooded her.

"Afraid so."

Christine finished the conversation and hung up, feeling mortified that she'd ever thought Chet had been a man worth moping over. And poor Sandy. He'd used her, too. Maybe he was running out of women who were willing to sell their ideas for his attention. A chill shivered down her back at the memories.

For a fleeting moment, Christine didn't care what happened. Her grandmother needed her for a while longer, and she wasn't budging until after Christmas.

She looked toward heaven asking for help. As prickles swept down her spine, a calm spread over her, and she knew the Lord had heard her prayers.

Will lifted his head when he heard a knock on the shop door. He laid down the copper foil and headed toward the sound. Christine stood at the window waving, and his heart squeezed, seeing her there with her nose pressed against the door's stained glass.

"This is a surprise," he said as she stepped inside.

She stomped the snow from her boots. "Linda came over with a new jigsaw puzzle and scooted me out of the house. She said she'd help with the therapy today. Grandma knows the routine, she just needs someone to keep an eye on her."

Will kissed the tip of her cold nose. "You sound like you feel guilty leaving her. You shouldn't."

"I know." She unbuttoned her coat and pulled the scarf from around her neck. "What are you doing?"

"A last-minute Christmas project. Everything else is finished." Just saying it, tension left his shoulders. "I love the work, but when I'm under a deadline, I feel the pressure."

"But you don't show pressure. That's what's so wonderful. I do. Chet's back today, and I have to call him this afternoon."

"What'll happen?"

"I don't know." He saw the confusion in her eyes before she lowered her head.

He drew her into his arms and nestled her against his chest. The snow from her jacket melted against his knit shirt, but her warmth compensated. "I've been thinking."

"About what?" She tilted her head upward to look at him.

"About your marketing ideas."

"Really?" Her eyes sparkled with anticipation.

"If you were here long enough to get me set up, maybe I could give it a try." The words seem to croak from his throat. "I'm nervous, I'll admit, and I'd start small. Maybe just jewelry and stained-glass boxes."

"You're really willing to give that a try?"

"Yes, but I need your help, and I won't know how to update the site. I'm not a graphic artist."

She brightened. "Neither am I, exactly, but I know enough about doing a Web site, and—"

"Did you hear what I said?" He gave her a squeeze.

"You have to be here to do that, and it will take some time."

She drew back, suspicion glowing on her face. "Are you doing this to keep me captive?"

"Not really, but that's a bonus."

She laughed, then gazed down at his shirt. "I got you all wet."

"I don't care." He drew her back into his arms, his mind flooding with things he wanted to say, but the store wasn't the place. "Have time for a ride?"

"Ride where?"

"Up the road. Maybe to Arch Rock."

"It's snowing."

"I know, and that makes it all the better."

She shrugged. "Sure, I'll go if it won't take too long."

"Let me grab my camera."

He hurried into the studio, slipped into his bib and realized Christine needed warmer clothing too. He grabbed his camera and tripod, then headed toward her.

"Let's go," he said, grasping her hand and leading her outside.

Soft flakes drifted from the sky, and the sun shone as if it had no idea it was winter. Will motioned to his sled. "Let's take mine," he said, "unless you prefer to drive yourself."

"No. I like riding with you."

She slipped into the seat and scooted back, making room for him. He dropped the tripod into the caboose and tucked the camera beneath his jacket, then started the engine.

"Here we go," he said, easing away from the curb, then headed down Market Street to the Fort Hill.

The wind whipped in his face, sending snowflakes shooting past like a torn feather pillow in a pillow fight. Christine leaned with him when they rounded the fort and raced up Arch Rock Road. He had an idea what he wanted to do, but his heart knotted in his throat. Now he had hope. If he spoke his mind, his hope could crumble.

At Arch Rock, the rugged bluff spread ahead of him like a fresh white sheet. Not one track blemished the pristine landscape. He hesitated, not wanting to mar the beauty. Instead, he pulled to the side of the road. "Look at that," he said, motioning to the expanse of white that stretched along the bluff.

He took Christine's hand and helped her from the sled, brushing the snow from her pants. With her hand in his, they walked along the bluff to Arch Rock, which towered one-hundred-and-fifty-feet into the air from the ground below and framed a scenic view of the Straits. Today the water's icy ripples glistened in the bright sun.

Will slipped his arm around Christine's shoulder. "What do you think of the view?"

"Wow! I've seen this in the summer, but there are no words to describe this."

He gave her a moment to enjoy the view, then turned her to face him. "There are no words to describe you, either."

Christine blinked, then smiled. "Thank you. I could say the same about you."

Will was captured by her gaze. Their eyes lingered, searching each other's faces as if time had stood still and the concerns and problems had faded beneath the mounds of crystals winking in the sunlight.

"Let me take your picture framed in the arch," he said. He didn't wait for a response, but darted back to the sled and grabbed his camera and tripod.

She argued, but he didn't listen and took her photograph with the sun glowing in her blond hair and a smile on her face, which brightened his world even more.

"That's enough," she said, shaking her head. "What's the tripod for?"

"For us." He opened its legs and attached the camera to the top. "Stay there, and I'll join you." He focused, set the lens, then the timer before darting to her side.

They stood in an embrace until the beeping stopped and a faint click reached his ears. "Now that didn't hurt, did it?"

Christine gave him a playful look. "Not at all, but I don't want to see myself on a calendar next year."

He wished she could be on every page of next year's edition.

Will took her hands and wove his fingers through hers. Though covered by gloves, he could feel the heat of her radiating through him. "Standing here with you is like a dream. Since you've been here—even when you didn't like me very much—you've captured my imagination, and I saw something inside you that I don't think you even knew was there."

She tilted her head as if trying to understand. "I'm sorry, Will. I guess I didn't like you very much. I was jealous of you, I think."

He grinned. "Jealous? That doesn't make sense. You have so much going for you."

"And you have so much going for you and with so much happiness. My grandmother knew you and loved you, and she barely knew me."

He saw the sadness in her face. "But she does now, and you're precious to her."

"I know, but I'm realizing that I've been longing for the day when I would feel truly confident and self-actualized."

Will reared back. "Now there's a five-dollar word."

"You know what I mean—reaching my potential—and I'm not sure that day will ever come the way I'm headed."

She looked up at him as if asking him to give her

the direction, and he knew it only came from the Lord. He shook his head, not knowing what to say.

"I'm praying, Will, and I'm looking for that direction you keep telling me about."

"Do you have faith that God will open the right door?"

"I do." She lowered her gaze. "I'm trying, too."

He heard her intake of breath, and she seemed to rally.

"Yes, I do, Will. You and Grandma can't be wrong."

He drew her closer, his laughter vibrating against her. She rested in his arms, looking at him. His gaze lingered on her mouth. He wanted to kiss her yet needed to speak his mind.

"Christine, I brought you here to this special place, because this is how I see you—pure and perfect. You stepped into my life such a short time ago, and I feel as if I've known you a lifetime."

He watched her eyes shift, exploring his as if trying to understand.

"I realize in such a short time, you can't make a life commitment, but Christine, I want to tell you that I love you. I know it in my soul."

Her head jerked back as if his declaration had startled her.

"Don't speak right now," he said, "but I think I should tell you how much I care about you, and if I had my way, you'd give us the time to get to know each other and to see where it leads. I know I've been led to you."

Tears rimmed her eyes. She closed them and opened them again, but she didn't pull away. Instead, she seemed to cling to him with anticipation. "I've dreamed of you saying these things to me. I fought the feelings for so long, but I've lost the battle."

"Christine, I—"

"No. Let me finish. But you're saying this at the worst time. I have to call Chet, and I'm not sure what's going to happen. I'm scared—scared to the depth of my being. My work has been my life, and I don't know if I can give it up."

She began to shake in his arms, and he had to lean closer to hear the next sentence.

An exhale rattled from her. "But I don't know if I can give you up, either."

"You can't give up on us, Christine. It's not you or me. It's us. Just give us time."

"I want to," she said. "I really want to."

He lowered his lips to hers, her icy mouth warming as his lips moved on hers. He heard her sigh, and his own sigh wove around it. The kiss deepened, and he knew in his heart that Christine could not walk away.

"I love you," he whispered into her hair.

"I don't deserve you."

Her words disappointed him. He'd longed to hear her say those three words that had never meant so much to him as now.

A cold wind lashed against his back, and he lifted his gaze as a cloud hid the sun. "We'd better go."

She nodded, stepping out from his arms and heading back to the sled.

His own thoughts felt as dark as the suddenly dusky sky. He'd told her the truth, and she'd left him feeling empty.

Chapter Sixteen

"I know I've made mistakes," Chet said. "I made you promises that I didn't keep. We need to talk, Christine."

"We are talking," she said, her fingers trembling against the telephone.

"Not on the phone. I need to see you in person. I have plans, and I need you here."

She shook her head. "I can't come, Chet. Not now. Christmas is in five days. I can't leave my grandmother now."

"Just come back for a couple of days. You can go back on the weekend. This is important. I have a promotion lined up for you, but I don't want to talk about it this way."

"A promotion? You're kidding." She'd waited so long to hear this.

"I talked to the vice president at corporate. He gave me the go-ahead."

"Can't you tell me about it on the phone?"

"No. I'm in a little spot here, and I need to know you're serious about this. If you can't take time for me, then how can I trust that you'll give your all to this job? I put in good words for you, Christine. You can't let me down now."

His offer spun in her head. A promotion. She'd lived and breathed that dream for so long. Chet could make it a reality. "For just two days?"

"Sure. You can go back for Christmas if you must, and then make arrangements for January. We need you here. *I* need you here."

"I'll leave in the morning, Chet. I have to make arrangements for my grandmother's care."

"Good girl, Christine. You won't be sorry. You're my girl, right?"

A gnawing feeling rolled down her spine. "I'll be there tomorrow morning."

When she hung up, her world spun out of control. Promotion? Will? She had to decide. Life as she knew it or life as she'd lived it the past few weeks?

Christine drew in a lengthy breath. Leaving was such bad timing. She had gifts to wrap, Christmas dinner to plan, her grandmother's care. Two days. All she could do was try to get back on Friday. That would give her Saturday and Sunday. Monday was Christmas Day.

* * *

Christine bent to kiss her grandmother's cheek. "I'll be back Friday night, I hope. If not, Saturday morning. You'll be okay, right?"

Her grandmother's eyes looked questioning. "I'll be fine, Christine. It's you I'm worried about."

Surprised, Christine stepped back. "Don't worry about me. The plane ride is short."

"I'm not concerned about the plane ride. I'm worried about you."

Christine knew what she'd meant, but the candid comment still startled her. She tensed, feeling everyone was against her. Will's reaction had been unpleasant. He'd tried to accept her decision, but she knew him well enough now to know he was upset.

Looking through the front window, Christine saw the taxi stop in front. "It's time to go."

Her grandmother craned her neck to look out the window. "Will's not taking you to the airport?"

"No. I didn't want to bother him. I called a taxi." Christine looked outside, watching steam from the horse's nostrils billow into the morning air.

"Linda's dropping by to help with your therapy, and she'll help you in the morning and at night. Will's a phone call away, and some of your ladies will be dropping by for lunch today and tomorrow. Will's agreed to handle dinner."

"You didn't have to do all that. I have to get along on my own now."

Her subtle comment made Christine cringe. The meaning didn't need explanation. "I'll be back Friday night," she said again.

She wrapped the scarf around her neck, remembering that Will had given it to her shortly after she'd arrived on the island. She fingered the fabric, then lifted her overnight case and headed out the front door.

The driver helped her into the carriage, and the horses swayed, then jerked forward, clopping along the snow-covered road. The frosty wind sneaked through the crevices of the rig, and she pulled the blanket over her legs, recalling how Will had tucked her in the day she arrived. She'd had such a bad attitude that day.

Only a few weeks had made a tremendous difference in the way she looked at life. She'd grown accustomed to the easygoing manner that belonged to the people who lived here.

She shivered again as warm tears blurred her vision. How could she turn down a promotion? She knew her grandmother and Will were disappointed. She saw it in their faces and heard it in their voices, but she'd be foolish not to listen to Chet's proposal.

The scenery flickered past, a blend of sun and shadow, almost like the emotions that racked her. The city awaited her. The city. Memories of creeping traffic on the freeways as snow and ice made driving treacherous—cars spinning out of control and vehicles sliding through lights and stop signs—accidents waiting to happen.

Her thoughts faded as the taxi turned into the airport driveway, the lengthy stretch to the terminal and airstrip. She'd be back tomorrow night. The trip wasn't that long and her grandmother would be fine.

The driver helped Christine alight and handed her the overnight bag, then climbed onto the carriage and jingled away.

As she turned, the sound of a sled roared behind her and she looked over her shoulder. Will. She stopped, her pulse charging through her.

He climbed from the sled and hurried to her side. "Do you know what you're doing?"

Will's question startled her. "Why would you ask, Will? I explained yesterday. I—" What was she doing? She looked into his disappointed face, his sparkling eyes shrouded with anguish. "It's the promotion I've always wanted. It's—"

"His lies. His manipulation. You might think he's changed, but he hasn't." He grasped her arms, his gaze riveted to hers. "But I can't make you love me."

Her chest ached. She did love him, but—

"I've said I love you, Christine, and I've tried to show you how I feel. I can't do any more. If you leave, your words have meant nothing. Remember our words belie our actions."

"I'll be back tomorrow, Will."

"Not really. You're already gone, Christine, and it

breaks my heart." He pulled her to him and pressed his warm lips against hers, the only warmth that touched her body at that moment.

He released her and spun away before she could think. The engine roared, and with blurred vision, she watched the sled make a turn and fly down the road.

Christine stood a moment until the sled vanished, her heart as empty as the landscape in front of her. She turned toward the terminal, her legs weak as she entered the building.

In a daze, she passed through the boarding gate and onto the tarmac, stepping onto the plane and settling into her seat. She sat a moment, trying to control the tears that welled in her eyes, the throbbing in her temple.

Snowflakes drifted past the window, and she looked out at the diamond-clad snow.

I brought you here to this special place, because this is how I see you—pure and perfect. Will's words whispered in her ear. Her chest tightened again, picturing his disappointed expression.

I feel as if I've known you a lifetime. She felt the same—his smile, his strong arms holding her close, his faith. A man any woman would give the world for had told her that he loved her.

A knot twisted in Christine's throat. Her eyes blurred again as she looked out at the landscape.

Chet's words blasted into her thoughts. *I have a*

promotion lined up for you. I talked to the vice president at corporate. He gave me the go-ahead.

She could still hear his voice. He sounded desperate. Just as she suspected, Chet was in trouble. He'd admitted it. "I'm in a little spot here," he'd said. She'd heard that line before and all his promises before.

The plane's engine revved as fear prickled down Christine's back. What was she doing? Will's words roared in her ears. *His lies. His manipulation. You might think he's changed, but he hasn't.*

She'd hurt Will to the core, but a promotion. Her dream. Her goal. Her life. Her—

Chet's voice rang in her ears. *I need to know you're serious about this. If you can't take time for me, then how can I trust that you'll give your all to this job? I put in good words for you, Christine. You can't let me down now.*

How can I trust you? Yes, and how could she trust him? Tears rolled down her cheeks. What had she done? Will's anguished face. Her grandmother's expression. She'd hurt them. Terribly. *Oh Lord, help me*, she moaned.

Will looked at his watch and climbed from his sled. He gazed into the sky and saw a plane above the treetops heading for St. Ignace. His heart felt void. He'd trusted and loved, and now he knew he could never trust her again.

He headed into the house, left his jacket in his

apartment, and took a deep breath before he opened the door into Grandma Ella's house. He had no spirit to work today. Earlier he'd tried, thinking it would fill his mind, but he'd cut a piece backward, and he'd burned his hand on the soldering iron. His race to the airport had done nothing more than open the wound even deeper.

When he stepped into the living room, Grandma Ella looked up, her face expectant, then sinking to despair. "You're back early," she said.

"I couldn't concentrate." He plopped onto the sofa and stretched his legs along the cushion, ashamed to admit he'd chased Christine to the airport with only a rejection for his efforts.

Will eyed Ella again and noticed she held the Bible in her hand. He'd prayed, but apparently God had other plans for him. He knew the Lord sometimes said no to prayers.

"Any good words for me in there?" he said, motioning toward the Bible.

She lifted her head and gave him a feeble smile. "All the words are good for us."

He nodded and looked away.

"But I did read something that you might need to hear." She opened the Bible and scanned the page. "It's in Proverbs, Chapter three—'Trust in the Lord with all your heart and lean not on your own understanding; in all your ways acknowledge Him, and He will make your paths straight.'"

Straight where? Will asked himself. Straight into the pits. He didn't respond but thought again of the words. *Lean not on your own understanding.* How could a person not try to understand? Today he felt stripped of hope. Not faith, but hope.

"God answers in His time, Will." As if she'd heard his thoughts, Grandma Ella's voice penetrated the silence.

"I know." He slipped his legs off the sofa and leaned his elbows on his knees, his hands knotted between them. "I really thought she loved me."

"She does, Will. I'm sure of it."

"I'm younger. I know that bothered her more than anything else."

"Age is nothing. She knows that. Age is of the heart, not the years."

He managed a grin. "You're a prime example of that."

"Eventually the years catch up with the body, but the heart knows no age."

"I feel empty inside." He shook his head. "I wish I'd given her the surprise I'd planned." His throat closed as he pictured the special Christmas gift he had for her.

Ella closed the Bible and slid it onto the table. "She'll be back tomorrow. She'll be here for Christmas."

He raised a hand and ran it through his hair. "It's not the same. The gift has no meaning now."

"All gifts have meaning."

A tear escaped his eyes and dripped on his hand. He brushed it away, not wanting Ella to notice. "Can I help you with your therapy?"

"Later." She leaned her head back and closed her eyes. "A little later."

"Okay," he said, staring at the carpet pattern, thinking that his life had gone from delight to heart-ache in the blink of an eye. He lifted his legs back onto the sofa and closed his eyes.

Sunlight and snow filled him. Christine's face glowing in the wintry air, framed by the Arch Rock. He felt his heart wrench. Christine nestled on his lap by the fireside. Christine watching him work in the studio. His plans, his dreams, his hopes shriveled away like autumn leaves.

Should he blame her? Advertising was her career. It was her livelihood. It was her pride and identity. If he loved her, how could he ask her to give that up for him?

Though he asked the question, he had no answer. He just wanted her to love him so much that a career didn't matter. Foolish notion. Could he give up his art? Art pumped within him like life-giving blood. He paused. The island. He could give up the island.

He opened his eyes again and stared at the ceiling. He'd miss the place. He loved the island res-idents' sense of community. He loved the quiet nights, the landscape brimming with natural beauty.

Yet he could live in the city if living there meant being with Christine.

They needed to talk. He checked his watch. Did she have her cell phone turned on? She was only a call away, but he'd wait, wait to make sure she'd landed safely.

Will rose and took quiet steps across the room. He gazed out the window, seeing the morning sun rising higher for another bright day. In his peripheral vision, he saw a carriage on the road. A taxi. His heart skipped. Christine? Hope filled his mind.

The driver slowed and stopped, then opened the carriage door. Will's pulse raced. He ran through the foyer and to the front door. Flinging it open, he bounded down the steps.

Christine dropped her carry-on onto the snow and flung herself into his arms. The feel of her clinging to him, the smell of her hair, the touch of her skin melded into a blessing. Her tear-wet lips touched his, and he felt her shudder in his arms.

"I'm sorry," she cried. "I've been a fool."

"No. You came back." He kissed the tears from her cheeks while his fingers caressed her hair, her neck, her cheek. "I love you, Christine. I'll go back to the city with you if you want. I can't lose you now."

"I don't want the city. I want you, and I want the island."

He lifted her in his arms and spun her around as the snow-white world blurred into a sunlit panorama.

The carriage moved away, and Will set Christine down to earth, afraid to let her go. Only the cold penetrating his shirt assured him this was not a dream but reality.

"I love you," she said, her eyes searching his.

"That's what I've wanted to hear," he said, swinging her into his arms and carrying her toward the house.

The scent of turkey and stuffing threaded through the room and drew Will from his apartment. The past four days had been beyond his dreams. He'd heard Christine say "I love you" more times than he had ever hoped, and the words meant as much each time he heard them.

Grandma Ella's face had beamed with joy when she saw Christine come through the door. She'd begun praising God from the moment Christine hurried to her arms. Will's heart had been in his throat.

"Is it time for a taste test?" Will asked, coming through the kitchen door. Christine stood with her back to him, pulling the turkey from the oven. He loved seeing Grandma Ella standing nearby helping with the preparations. She had to watch her balance and force her left hand to function, but he could tell she'd nearly become her old self.

He gave the elderly woman a kiss on the cheek as he sneaked past and tore a sliver of turkey from the bird.

Christine gave him a playful smack, then pointed to the electric knife. "Start cutting, and that's an order."

He grinned, wanting to kiss her cream-colored neck where she'd pinned her hair up for church. She wore one of Grandma Ella's aprons tied over her deep purple dress. He looked down to see her in fuzzy slippers.

"I like your outfit," he said, nodding toward her footwear.

She ignored him, and he decided the faster he sliced the turkey the quicker they'd eat. He couldn't wait to open gifts, and he was positive his would be a surprise.

Christine's mind flew between preparing the meal, thinking of her amazing journey with Will, then sinking to an abyss when she thought about her conversations with Chet.

The call had been difficult, but when she'd hung up, she'd walked away with confidence. She had nothing to lose anymore by letting corporate know the truth about Chet—how he'd used his charm and idle promises on unsuspecting female coworkers to gain his own success. She'd pondered whether her action was vindictive, but Grandma Ella had convinced her—and Will had agreed—the sinner needed to repent to be forgiven, and Chet had yet to learn that lesson.

When the food was ready, she called everyone to the dining room table set with her grandmother's Christmas dinnerware. As always, they joined hands for prayer.

"Lord," her grandmother began, "we thank You for this day and especially for Your guidance. Nothing could bring me more joy, Father, than to have Christine and Will here together with Your blessing. Help us to always trust Your will and follow the path You make for us to follow. We ask you to bless this food to our body, and we thank You for the gift of Your Son who gives us eternal life. We pray this in Jesus's precious name."

"Amen," Christine said, joining the others, but her amen came with a feeling of relief and joy. She'd finally understood the closeness with the Lord that Will had often talked about. God had guided her off the plane and back into a taxi rather than fly the meaningless journey to Southfield. Life's meaning was right here on the island.

Once the plates were filled, the conversation moved to the two worship services they'd attended both yesterday and that morning, Christine's parents, and plans for the future.

"I have to go back in January and move my things here. Eventually, I'll need to look for an apartment or—"

"You'll do no such thing," her grandmother said. "I'd be delighted for you to stay with me if you would until—"

"Grandma, I'd love to stay here. This house means so much to me. It always holds good memories, and—"

"And here's my gift to you if you'll take it with good intention," Ella said.

Christine lifted her head and lowered her fork. "Gift?" She grinned.

"Maybe this is presumptuous of an old woman, but this house is too big for me. If you decide to stay for good—" She glanced from her to Will. "I'd love to trade. You can enjoy the house, and I'll fit as snug as a bug in the apartment. I want you to have this house, and I know your parents would agree. But if I'd be in your way, then I could—"

"Grandma," Christine said, "you'll never be in my way. If it weren't for you, I'd be sitting in Southfield right now, listening to Chet's lies." She looked at Will. "I knew I loved Will, but like that children's poem, 'The Spider and The Fly,' I was ready to fall into Chet's web again, because I'm too stupid and naive."

"You're too trusting and honest," Will said. "You want to believe, and Chet won't let you."

She reached across the cloth to grasp Will's hand. "I'm ashamed at the things I let worry me. Age. My work. Island life. After I quit fighting, those things meant nothing, and anyway, I have a new job, and I'm excited."

"You have a new job?" Grandma Ella's voice lifted in surprise.

"I'm going to build a Web site for Will and be his webmaster and new marketing director."

"That's wonderful, Christine," her grandmother

said, her eyes shifting toward Will as if making sure he was pleased.

"Speaking of gifts, it's gift time," Will said, standing up and pushing in his chair.

His abrupt announcement surprised Christine. "We have to clean up first."

"That can wait, but this can't."

"Why not?"

"I'm too excited." Will caught her elbow and beckoned her to follow.

Confused, she studied her grandmother to see if she knew anything about the surprise, but she looked at her and didn't blink.

Will captured her hand and tugged her through the back door to the porch. She stared ahead, looking at the snow, and wrapped her arms around herself to fend away the cold. "What?"

"Look there," he said, pointing toward the driveway.

When she turned, her heart leaped. "It's a new snowmobile, and what's that in the seat?"

"Your bib."

"You bought me a snow outfit and a sled? But you didn't know if—"

"I have faith," he said, slipping his arms around her cold shoulders. "I won the sled at the Christmas bazaar draw."

"The one at Doud's?" She frowned. "But you told me—"

"It was won by a year-round resident, and that's

right. Me. I had Jude keep it at his place, and I sneaked it here this morning after church."

"I can't believe this. You're giving it to me." She looked him in the eyes, amazed at what he'd said. "You really knew I'd stay."

"I hoped with all my heart."

"Your faith is so strong." She tiptoed to give him a quick kiss.

"Yours, too," he said, turning her toward the warmth of the house. "You came back, didn't you?"

She'd come back—back home, and she never wanted to leave.

Chapter Seventeen

Seven Weeks Later

"The ice bridge is ready," Will called as he came into the house, anxious to see Christine.

She pivoted toward him from the table. "What's that mean?"

"We can ride to St. Ignace. Solid ice from here to there."

She scooted back the chair. "You mean we can actually take the sleds over."

"That's exactly what I mean."

He walked up behind her and put his cold hands on her warm neck.

She scrunched her neck into her shoulders. "That's not fair."

"Maybe not, but this is." He kissed her neck and

then swept back her hair to kiss her cheek, enjoying the sweetness of her fragrance.

"What this?" he asked, when he looked at the computer.

"It's the Web site."

"Really?" He pulled up a chair beside her.

"This is the home page. It's a picture of the shop. Later I'll take one without the snow. And here's the picture I took inside."

"Nice," he said, amazed to see the detail of her photograph. "I can see the window I just hung."

She moved the cursor. "Here's the links. This one says Shop Online. The shopper will click here and I'll have categories of your products. And this will be good for people coming to the island or people who are browsing the Internet."

He hated to quell her excitement. "That's great, Christine, but—"

"I know," she said, hitting the close button and turning off the computer. "You want to go out on the ice bridge."

The fact that she'd sensed what he wanted gave him a good feeling. "Yes, but before we leave, I have a surprise for you." He stepped back and pulled a sheet of something from beneath his jacket.

She eyed it a moment until he handed it to her. Her heart lurched, seeing the amazing photograph of her red glove putting her last initial in the pristine snow. W. L. + C. P. Beneath the photo was Will's name and the title "Love on Cupid's Pathway." Love had come to her in this lovely place. "Your photo made it this time?"

"It did. And all because of those pretty red gloves."

Her eyes blurred with happiness as she wrapped her arms around Will's neck. "It was your sensitive photography."

He kissed the end of her nose. "It was that and love on Cupid's Pathway."

She grinned at his silliness and studied the photo again, so proud that he'd finally had a winning entry in the calendar contest.

"Okay. Enough of this flattery. Let's take a ride. I want to get there before it gets dark." He gave her another hug. "Get ready, and I'll meet you outside."

"Give me a minute. I want to see if someone will come and stay with Grandma."

"We'll only be gone an hour or so. She can probably stay alone. Take the cell phone."

"I'll check with her," she said. She handed him the photograph, and he headed for the door to his apartment.

Inside his rooms, he slipped on his bib, then put on his jacket and zipped it. He slid the smock over his head and grabbed his helmet.

Christine had never experienced the ice bridge and had no idea what a relief this was to those who resided on the island. The ice had frozen enough to hold the sleds and the residents were free to zip over to St. Ignace for shopping or appointments, even go to a movie without paying the ferry or plane fare.

He opened the door to the house. "Ready?"

Footsteps banged down the stairs, and Christine appeared, bundled in her bib and jacket, her feet bound in boots. "I feel like a jumbo baby-blue pillow," she said, carrying her mittens and earmuffs.

"But a beautiful jumbo pillow," he said, giving her a gentle kiss.

"Grandma said she'd be fine, but I'll call her in a half hour or so just to make sure."

"She'll be great," he said, touched by Christine's concern.

Outside, Christine climbed onto her new, larger sled, but she looked confident. She'd caught on to sledding faster than the speed of Shepler's hydroplanes that brought visitors to the island.

He settled onto his sled, wishing Christine was tucked behind him, but he couldn't deny her the fun of driving her new sled. "Let's go," he said, motioning her forward.

The sleds pulled out to the driveway, but Christine halted. "Does the bridge begin downtown?"

"No, the British Landing. That's where the bridge has been marked out."

They sped onto the road, the wind in their faces, and headed up Hoban to Annex Road, then British Landing Road. He glanced behind him to see Christine smiling beneath her helmet. She waved, and he waved back.

When they arrived, he waited for her to catch up. "See the trees." He pointed to the line of discarded Christmas trees that residents used to mark the bridge.

"Somewhere along here are our trees," she said.

"It keeps us on the sure path for the sleds and pedestrians."

"Pedestrians?"

"Some people have the courage to walk the four miles across the ice." He leaned over and grasped her hand to kiss her glove.

"You're silly."

"Only when I'm with you.

"Look," she said, pointing across the frozen water. "The sun is setting."

He looked at the horizon, seeing the muted colors—corals, purples and golds reflected in the snow and ice. "It's like a rainbow almost."

"A promise." She squeezed his hand.

"We'd better go."

"Into the sunset," she called as he pulled ahead of her onto the ice.

Christine followed, gliding up alongside with a wide smile. The Christmas trees lying along the pathway flashed by, and once he was halfway across, he slowed.

"Let's stop and get out here," he said. He parked to the side in case another sled came along.

He climbed out, and Christine pulled behind him. He grasped her hand to help her off the sled onto the ice.

"Here we are standing on the Straits of Mackinac," he said, amazed at the thrill he had each time he experienced it.

Christine did a full turn and swung back with her face beaming. "It's awesome."

He took her hand and pulled off her glove to feel her warm flesh in his. "Not as awesome as you are."

"I love this place, Will—the island and the people."

Will broke into laughter. "If I remember correctly, you offered to cook me a seven-course dinner or whatever I choose if I ever heard you say that you loved it here."

"I did?"

He brushed her cheek. "I love food, as you know, but I have something else I love much better."

Her eyes narrowed, then she gave him a crooked grin. "You look guilty…like you have something up your sleeve."

"Nothing up my sleeve." He paused, his heart thundering beneath his down-filled jacket. "But I do have something in my pocket."

She frowned and followed his hand as he dug inside and pulled out the small velvet box.

Her eyes widened, and he handed it to her. She stood a moment, staring at the lid as if she were unable to move.

"Will." She looked at him, then the box.

"Open it," he said.

Christine inched the lid upward and peeked inside. The cathedral setting with its row of paved cut diamonds on each side of a princess-cut stone glistened in the setting sunlight. "It's beautiful. Gorgeous."

"You're far more beautiful."

He removed the ring from the box and knelt down on the frigid ice. "Christine, maybe you think I should wait, but I love you now, and I know our love will grow and grow with God's blessing. Will you be my wife?"

Her cheeks trembled as she looked down at him. Tears welled in her eyes, and she nodded. "Yes. Yes. I'll love you forever."

He rose, slipped the ring on her finger and drew her into his arms. Their lips met, and warmth spread through him into his heart.

Christine yielded to his kiss, her arms wrapping around his neck, her body straining upward on tiptoes to offer her love. She'd told him once he had Christmas in his heart, and today Christine filled it to the brim.

She had her own mind and plans, but God had given her path a turn and led her straight into his arms.

* * * * *

Dear Reader,

Mackinac Island is one of my favorite Michigan vacation spots. If you have never been there, it is well worth the effort to make the trip. As soon as you leave the passenger ferry and step onto Main Street, you will be greeted by the scent of the famous Mackinac Island fudge and their wonderful caramel corn. I'd enjoyed the island in every season except winter, so I had fun researching the island in winter with the help of a year-round resident. Life on the island is very much as I described it—a world of horse and carriage, bicycles, walking and snowmobiles in winter. I've had the pleasure of staying at the island's most renowned hotel, the Grand Hotel, where the movie *Somewhere in Time* was filmed.

I chose this wonderful island to share a spiritual lesson we all need to remember and one of which we are all guilty—making our own plans without asking God's direction or without asking His purpose for us. How often have we acted without asking *Is this what the Lord would have us do?* Christine was so certain her success would bring her happiness and contentment. She had spent her life planning her course, but forgot that it is the Lord who guides her steps. With Will's support and with the power of the Holy Spirit, Christine learned that happiness and contentment are gifts from God. In Him, we can find true love and true happiness.

Sometimes the Lord's direction is only a small voice in our heads or a feeling in the core of our being, and if we aren't patient and listen, we may miss the Lord's will or the wonderful talents and gifts He's given us to use for Him. I pray that you and I listen carefully for God's guidance.

Gail Gaymer Martin

QUESTIONS FOR DISCUSSION

1. Island life is different. What do you see as the pros and cons of island living?

2. Christine's attitude changed from the beginning of the book to the end. What do you think caused those changes? Have you ever experienced something that has changed your life?

3. Will knew he had disappointed his parents. Have you ever felt as if you disappointed your parents? Your family? How did their disappointment affect you?

4. Elderly people have a knack for getting away with bluntness. How do you see this played out in Grandma Ella's conversations?

5. Christine felt that God didn't answer her prayer. Have you ever felt that God didn't answer your prayers? Discuss praying and what we should expect from God.

6. Age difference is a factor in this story. Grandma Ella said the Bible does not designate who has to be older or younger in a marriage. Do you have any feelings about age differences? If so, what are they and why?

7. This book is filled with Christmas activities and traditions. Which traditions do you enjoy with your family? Are any of yours different from what was experienced in the book?

8. Sexual harassment in the workplace is not uncommon. Chet's behavior was a form of harassment. Have you experienced any forms of sexual harassment? How did it affect you?

9. Christine mentioned how subliminal messages are used in advertising. Can you think of times that people in everyday life say something with a hidden message underneath the words?

10. The theme of this book is Proverbs 16:9— In his heart a man plans his course, but the Lord determines his steps. How many examples of this can you find in the story? Can you see this verse having meaning in your own life?

Love Inspired

LOVE WALKED IN
BY
MERRILLEE WHREN

Getting close to new neighbor Clay Reynolds was not a consideration for single mom Beth Carlson. She had no time for romance. Clay was good to her son—and to her—but she could never give her heart to a motorcycle-riding man again. Or could she?

Available December 2006, wherever you buy books.

Steeple Hill®

www.SteepleHill.com

LILWI

REQUEST YOUR FREE BOOKS!

2 FREE INSPIRATIONAL NOVELS
PLUS 2
FREE
MYSTERY GIFTS

Love Inspired®

YES! Please send me 2 FREE Love Inspired® novels and my 2 FREE mystery gifts. After receiving them, if I don't wish to receive any more books, I can return the shipping statement marked "cancel." If I don't cancel, I will receive 4 brand-new novels every month and be billed just $3.99 per book in the U.S., or $4.74 per book in Canada, plus 25¢ shipping and handling per book and applicable taxes, if any*. That's a savings of at least 20% off the cover price! I understand that accepting the 2 free books and gifts places me under no obligation to buy anything. I can always return a shipment and cancel at any time. Even if I never buy another book from Steeple Hill, the two free books and gifts are mine to keep forever.

113 IDN EF26   313 IDN EF27

Name _____ (PLEASE PRINT)

Address _____ Apt. _____

City _____ State/Prov. _____ Zip/Postal Code _____

Signature (if under 18, a parent or guardian must sign)

Order online at www.LoveInspiredBooks.com

Or mail to Steeple Hill Reader Service™:

IN U.S.A.	IN CANADA
P.O. Box 1867	P.O. Box 609
Buffalo, NY	Fort Erie, Ontario
14240-1867	L2A 5X3

Not valid to current Love Inspired subscribers.

Want to try two free books from another series?
Call 1-800-873-8635 or visit www.morefreebooks.com

* Terms and prices subject to change without notice. NY residents add applicable sales tax. Canadian residents will be charged applicable provincial taxes and GST. This offer is limited to one order per household. All orders subject to approval. Credit or debit balances in a customer's account(s) may be offset by any other outstanding balance owed by or to the customer. Please allow 4 to 6 weeks for delivery.

LIREG06

TITLES AVAILABLE NEXT MONTH

Don't miss these four stories in December